Ben Hiant, Ardnamurchan

AT the very western point of mainland Scotland, hugged on three sides by the Atlantic, lies the Ardnamurchan penin___. From Ben Hiant, the holy hill, can be seen spectacular v___ e Hebrides.

The land here has had a troubled history, w___ ___ ___ earances of villages for the more profitable sheep. ___ ___ Mingary.

Still, its wonderful beaches promis___ ___ ___ ore peaceful holiday!

£5.99

People's Friend Annual

Dear Reader,

A warm welcome to the wonderful "Friend" Annual for 2006. You have a real treat in store! We have 25 brand-new stories from all of your "Friend" favourites, and whether you are in the mood for romance, nostalgia or a bit of amusement, you're sure to find it here.

We take our usual trip round Britain with the beautiful paintings of J. Campbell Kerr, and we look to the past with three of our most popular poets, Brenda G. Macrow, Kathleen O'Farrell and Maggie Smith, who recall the joys of a Sunday afternoon out.

As well as our scenic views, this year we take a culinary tour of Britain to partake of some delicious local dishes!

So settle down, put your feet up, and spend some quality time with your "Friend"!

The Editor

Complete Stories

p142

Sunday Afternoon Out

p155

Cookery Around The British Isles

4

2006 Contents

p119

p62

J. Campbell Kerr Paintings

p161

Happy New Year!

by Mary Scott.

Illustration by Richard Eraut.

"NICK, won't you change your mind? Come on, please. It's not too late."

Jessica Rutherford stood, her open suitcase on the bed before her, looking pleadingly at her boyfriend.

Nick sat in the chair, his long legs slung over its arm, hands linked behind his head, watching her pack. His expression was amiable, but he shook his head in response to her coaxing.

"Jess, love, you know I can't. There's one or two things coming up and I can't afford to miss out on work, now can I?" He grinned at her.

"You should be pleased with me. Haven't you been saying that it's time I was more serious about work?"

Jess stuffed the last item roughly into the case and tried to speak reasonably.

"You know perfectly well that what I meant was it's time to try to get something real, something permanent. How can we possibly sort out our life together when you can be out of work for months at a time?"

Nick looked unrepentant.

"You mean acting isn't real work? Well, blow me. If it weren't for acting we would never have met, let me remind you. Anyway, don't you have your great nine-to-five office job now?"

Jess scowled at him.

"I have no intention of subsidising you while you spend all day watching soaps in your tip of a flat and all evening in the pub gossiping with your fellow unemployed thespians. Oops, sorry, I mean resting, of course.

"You said you wanted us to get married, didn't you? Suppose we have a baby? I'm an old-fashioned girl as far as that goes. I'd want to take care of my baby myself."

Nick sat up.

"Well, we haven't got a baby, have we?"

"No, and there's no chance we ever will if this goes on!" Jess blinked, feeling a sudden need to cry.

"Oh, well — if you won't, you won't, I suppose." She managed a brighter tone. "Too bad you'll miss my mother's feast for the New Year party. You know how she loves the way you can pack away her food!"

Nick patted his slim midriff. He could eat and eat without gaining an ounce.

"Too true, and don't you think for a minute I haven't considered what I'm missing. But work is work, and I mean to be hard-working in the new year. I'll make you proud of me yet."

Jess couldn't help a reluctant smile sneaking on to her face. He could almost always win her over.

"Oh, cut it out and help me get this stuff out to the car. And make sure you look in here every day to water my plants!"

JESS had covered much of the distance between London and her northern home before she felt able to focus on what lay ahead rather than thinking back towards Nick. It was as if a cord tying her to him were unwinding behind her, tugging her heart backwards. She had brooded on the situation as she competently negotiated the motorway.

Nick was right when he said that acting had brought them together. If he hadn't had a small part in the drama series that had been set in her picturesque home village, Jess would never have met him.

In her mind, she could hear Nick speak reproachfully.

"Darling Jess, it was a small but important part."

She grinned to herself. He'd had the part of a very flirtatious postman who appeared in every episode. In fact, he'd hardly had to act — just be himself! He had taken the viewers' fancy, and had been inundated with fan mail as a result.

Of course, Jess reflected, she hadn't realised that Nick's career was still in its fledgling state. She had been bowled over by the whole experience of having the production team, film crew and actors taking over the normally quiet village.

It had changed the place, and not just at the time of the filming. Once its scenic charm had been revealed to an audience of millions the village had become a tourist hotspot, and the summer saw a stream of cars and tour buses passing through.

Many natives regretted the changes, but Jess had never looked back. She'd always wanted to be an actress, taking an enthusiastic part in school plays, and when she was hired as an extra in several episodes, she had been sure she was on the ladder to stardom.

Nick had encouraged her to give up all her plans to go to university and instead head south in pursuit of an acting career.

She'd always hated living in the country, the routine of the farm dictating everything they did, and the round of gossip that kept the small community amused. She couldn't wait to be away from it all. Her parents had been apprehensive, but willing to compromise by insisting Jess take a secretarial course at the local college before moving away.

A S she neared home, Jess began to think more of what was waiting for her. She hadn't been home since she had made the great decision to put her acting aspirations behind her and look for an office job.

It hadn't been easy, and she knew Nick hadn't approved, but rather to her own surprise, Jess had discovered that she loved having a proper routine. She revelled in the day-to-day company of her fellow workers and, most amazingly of all, had shown such aptitude that she had been quickly promoted.

Her parents had been delighted and, Jess thought, probably very relieved. They must have been worried about her, though they had always been supportive and encouraging. And what was more, they had never uttered a word of criticism about Nick.

Jess knew they liked him — well, they could hardly help it — but they must have wished that she'd fallen in love with someone who belonged in the world they knew.

And Jess knew that now it was time for her to decide once and for all whether she and Nick had any future together.

She couldn't help feeling that he was drifting away from her. Was it even true that he was staying in London over the holiday period? What producers would be casting then? Wasn't it more likely that he had been asked to join some house party in the south of France, or maybe to go with his friend Sandy on that diving holiday in the Red Sea? She knew Sandy had asked him more than once.

Nick, she reflected, was always in demand as an entertaining and charming guest.

Well, she would keep phoning him. If he changed his mind and came north, she would take that as a sign that she could commit herself wholeheartedly to the relationship. Being back home would give her a new perspective on things, she was sure.

NEXT morning, in crisp and gloriously sunny weather, she looked down on the valley from a vantage point high above her parents' farm. Despite the cold she'd wrapped up warm and set out on a walk to clear her head of mournful thoughts about Nick. Rebel, her dad's elderly and now retired sheepdog, had elected to accompany her, and his infectious pleasure in the outing was cheering.

The palest sapphire sky arched cloudless over the frost-bound valley. Sunlight glinted on the stubble in fields yet unploughed, trembled in the water of the little river, and sparkled from the gilded weathervane on the church spire.

It was all just as it always had been, and yet somehow different. Jess thought about that as she leaned on the field gate. The difference, she had to admit, was in herself.

Normally, she felt trapped by the isolation and grinding yearly round of the farm. Yet today she was enchanted by the winter beauty of the landscape and the serenity of the quiet fields and hills.

That she hated the place and wanted only to escape from it had been for so long a given factor in her thoughts that Jess could scarcely believe that, somehow, unnoticed and unremarked, these feelings had evaporated, vanishing like the frost on the fields where the sun's rays touched them.

Coming home had been unexpectedly cheering after the long, lonely drive, and the unreservedly warm welcome comforting after her worries about Nick.

After all, she thought, it's so lovely, and so blissfully quiet after London. If only Nick were here . . .

Her brother, Dan, and his family had come by to say hello, and Jess had found her hurt feelings soothed by the warmth of their hugs and the excitement of her little nieces. There was a lot to be said for family life — and that was something she hadn't appreciated before, either.

A tractor bumbled along the river road, pulling a trailer loaded with hay bales. It was the only movement in a hushed world, and Jess squinted, trying to identity the driver. Red hair, she thought, and youngish. Who on earth?

"Someone new in the valley, Reb?"

The dog yawned.

"Well, it could be interesting. Mum will know. Come on."

Her phone, tucked hopefully in her pocket, stayed mute, without call or message from Nick. Jess brooded on the reasons for his silence, but firmly told herself that she couldn't care less. She would try to make the most of this holiday, look up old friends, and maybe check out what or who was new on the local scene.

HAVE a scone, pet. You look nipped with the cold." The farmhouse kitchen was cosy; her mother was in the throes of a major baking session. "See anyone interesting when you were out?"

"Hardly. I walked up the hill — Rebel enjoyed it." Jess buttered a scone. "The only sign of life was a tractor on the river road."

"William Robb, that'd be." Her mother dusted some flour over her baking board. "He's overwintering some ewes in the river fields. You don't know him, Jess — he moved here after you went to London. He bought Dainhead after old Jock Parker retired."

Jess stirred her coffee.

"Is he nice?" She didn't really care, but it would please her mother if she asked.

Her mum flicked a glance at her daughter, wondering.

"Oh, very. Hard working, too. By the way, is Nick coming up for the New Year? You didn't say."

"Maybe." Jess frowned at her coffee mug. "It depends."

"Depends on what?"

Jessica looked up and met her mother's gaze squarely.

"On whether he finds something more amusing to do, I suppose."

"Oh, dear." Her mother paused, floury rolling-pin in hand. "Are you two not so — you know? Is something wrong?"

"We haven't actually been right for ages, not since I gave up dreaming about being a great actress and got real."

"But that's a grand job you have now."

"Yeah — but unfortunately nine to five doesn't fit in with Nick's way of life, Mum. He likes me to be ready to go at a moment's notice whenever the mood takes him.

"I've become too dull and stodgy for his liking. I've realised that I'm a good organiser, with an eye for detail and a liking for routine. And I hate all that superficial luvvie stuff that actors have to put up with." Jess paused. How true that was really hit her as she put it into words. But all the same . . .

"I do love Nick, despite everything. I'm still hoping he'll change his mind

10

The Sunday School Picnic

With children dressed in their Sunday best — on their best
  behaviour, too! —
And Vicar beaming on one and all, the way that vicars do,
While Mrs Dove runs to and fro,
(She teaches Sunday School, you know),
It means the longed-for day is here,
Our picnic — the highlight of the year!

And soon the trestle table's piled with luscious things to eat,
Sandwiches, sausage-rolls and buns, and every sort of treat,
Then Vicar cracks his little joke, the one he always makes,
Pretending he was up at dawn, baking fairy cakes,
But we all know, though we smile at his quip,
It was really the Women's Fellowship!

And oh, how eagerly we wait for Vicar to say Grace,
Such joy and such expectancy lighting up each face,
For then, washed down with lemonade, we set to, with a will,
Enjoying that delicious food, until we've had our fill.
And later, thanks to Mrs Dove, there are races to be run,
With jolly games for all to play, and prizes to be won . . .

I'm so glad I go to Sunday School and, be it sun or rain,
I'll never miss, be sure of this — till it's picnic time again!
                   — *Kathleen O'Farrell.*

and come for New Year. But —" she shrugged "— I'm not holding my breath."

Her mother smiled.

"He'll be very welcome if he comes. I've asked a good crowd this year, seeing you're home. All the family, of course, and plenty of the younger ones that you know from school — oh, and young William Robb, too, seeing he's new here."

Jess eyed her mother shrewdly. Was there just something too casual about the throwaway addition of the new man in the village?

Too bad if there was. Mum's wasting her time, Jess thought. I've had enough of romance. Maybe I've also had enough of life down south, but that doesn't mean I'm ready to be a country housewife either.

Driving back later into a rosy sunset after visiting her sister, Nancy, who was every bit the housewife that Jess had scorned, she stopped on the river road behind a flock of sheep.

Two collies were working the jostling mob, directed by a tall young man, broad shouldered in his ancient Barbour jacket, a cap pulled down over reddish-brown hair.

The new neighbour, Jess decided. And definitely not bad looking, if you liked the type.

HE turned as she moved very slowly behind the sheep. Then he came back to speak to her. Jess wound down the window. At close quarters she saw he had clear smooth skin and hazel eyes.

"Sorry to hold you up. Won't be long."

"No problem. You must be William Robb. I'm Jessica Rutherford — my dad farms Barnside, up on the hill."

"Oh, right. You must be the daughter from London. He said you were coming home for the New Year."

Jess felt his glance was disparaging. She was dressed smartly, having a horror of coming home to collapse into woolly cardies and welly boots.

"That's me — the city slicker!"

He looked blank.

"Well, I'd better crack on."

The flock surged into the field, the dogs at their heels, and William Robb moved on to close the gate. Jess pulled up alongside him.

"Hey, are you sure you should be putting them in there?"

His eyebrows raised, the young man looked at Jess. What do you know about it? The thought was clearly written on his face.

"I mean, that field's notorious for flooding. I've never seen sheep in there before."

"I know what I'm doing."

Jess shrugged.

"I may live in London, but I was raised here. Watch out if it rains heavily."

William Robb whistled up his dogs and strode off along the road.

Jess leaned out of the window to shout after him, irked by his curtness.

"Looking forward to seeing you at our New Year party — not!" she added more quietly as the broad shoulders vanished in the dusk without an answering wave.

AT tea, she quizzed her dad.

"Haven't you told that young guy that the field by the Long Pool floods badly? He was turning his lambing ewes into it when I came back from Nancy's."

Her dad grinned.

"Took kindly to being told, did he?"

"How do you know I told him?"

"You wouldn't have been able to help yourself."

Jess laughed.

"I got my nose bitten off for it."

"You can't tell some folk, can you? They have to learn for themselves." Her dad looked innocently over the edge of his cup at his younger daughter.

"Ouch." Jess acknowledged the hit, but declined to take it further. "I'm going to phone Nick and see if he's made his mind up about the New Year."

The conversation hardly smoothed her ruffled feathers.

"Darling, I adore you and your home, too, but here is where the action is. There are one or two things developing and one daren't take one's lovely face away for an instant, not even to feature in my favourite country soap."

Jess could picture him smiling as he parodied himself. Couldn't he just drop it for a moment? She needed him to listen.

"I do need to see you. Nick — I miss you." Jess waited, hoping against hope that there would be an immediate and warm response. When none was forthcoming, she sighed and continued.

"Mum's invited a crowd; she really hopes you'll come. Oh, and we have a new neighbour, a rather dishy chap. He'd take a star part in a country soap."

"Single, eligible and good-looking? Oh, lucky Jess!" Nick's laughter was warm and, unfortunately, in no way anxious. "So I'd better make tracks north before my girl is swept into the brawny arms of this country yokel?"

Jess abandoned her attempt to keep calm.

"Oh, suit yourself, Nick. As you will, I've no doubt."

She was still smarting when she chanced to run into William Robb again as she dashed across the main street in the village on Christmas Eve. Flakes of snow were spiralling lazily down, and his arms were full of parcels. She swerved to avoid him, he stepped sideways, too and, inevitably, they collided.

"Sorry!" Jess gathered up some of the things. "You've been busy."

"Christmas shopping. Very last minute. Listen, I'm glad to see you again. I've been thinking. I was very short with you the other day. I want to apologise."

Jess laughed.

"Unasked-for advice . . . who wants it? Not me, either."

"Let me buy you a coffee to make up. I really am looking forward to that party after all."

She was very casual when telling her mother later.

"I think I got the wrong impression the other day. He seems less abrasive than I thought."

"You got on better today then?" Her mother registered Jess's flushed cheeks and bright eyes.

"Mmm. I'm going to walk down and meet him at the pub tonight. He needs to get out more and meet some of the younger lot around here. He's hardly been off the farm since he got here."

Her mother looked flustered.

"What about Nick? If he phones, what will I tell him?"

Jess winked at her.

"Just say I'm out with the local yokel and see how he likes that."

Her mother wouldn't say anything so provocative, she knew, but it wouldn't do Nick any harm to be left wondering.

THOSE normally dull days between Christmas and New Year turned out to be much more fun than Jess had expected. William Robb was proving to be rather entertaining, and it was surprisingly easy to slip back into the company of her age group in the village.

Time flew by as she caught up with old friends, visited her brothers and sisters, and helped William out with chores. Seeing him regularly made Jess aware that it would be worryingly easy to fall for him.

He was very attractive, in his tall, outdoorsy way, with that mouth that seemed always on the verge of smiling. She could see, in the eyes of her friends, a readiness to regard William and herself as an item. If only that cord that linked her with the faraway Nick would break and set her free!

But still she felt the tug on her heart, pulling backwards in a way she now half resented but couldn't deny.

By the dawn of New Year's Eve the hard frost had broken and clouds slumped heavily across the hill tops. By lunchtime it had started raining, and the day was darkening fast.

Jess had given up all thought of Nick arriving unexpectedly. Up till now she had cherished the hope that he meant to turn up unannounced, but she had at

Dawlish

THIS sleepy Devon fishing village with its pleasant climate and beaches became popular in Regency times.

In 1803, the Lawn was laid out in the centre of town round the Dawlish Water, a little stream with waterfalls. The tranquil park is still here, with the addition of black swans, descendants of those gifted from Australia in 1937.

Add to that the three beaches, and the station on the main line to Penzance, and it's clear why this corner of Devon is still so popular with those who wish to get away from it all!

J. CAMPBELL KERR.

last admitted that it was increasingly unlikely.

She glammed up as much as possible in the evening and was rewarded by an appreciative gleam in William's eyes when he arrived at the party, already in full and noisy swing. It was a look that was balm to the hurt place in Jess's heart, and she gladly went into his arms to be swung into the dance.

Her dad waltzed past them and shouted in William's direction.

"Have you checked the river level, lad? There's been heavy rain on the hills."

"I looked as I came along," William shouted back, grinning. "The ewes were well up the field, sheltering behind the bales. The water's fast and up a bit but not too dangerous."

HE seemed unconcerned and enjoying the party but, by half-past eleven, with the rain still thundering down, William was admitting to some anxiety.

"Jess, I think I'll just nip down and take a look at those ewes. But I'll be back to claim a kiss at midnight."

"I'll come with you." Jess pulled out a jersey and raincoat from the hall cupboard, and pushed her feet into wellies.

They were on the point of leaving when the phone rang. Jess looked back and hesitated. Nick? Phoning from some glamorous venue, ready to laugh at her rustic boyfriend?

"Get it — a minute or two won't make any difference," William urged.

It *was* Nick. Jess tightened her lips. Too bad. He'd missed his chance. Yet, despite her hurt and anger, her heart skipped at the sound of his voice.

"Having a fun time in the city, Nick?"

"Not exactly." He was laughing. Then, in the background, she heard another sound. It couldn't be — she must be hearing things. Not unless they'd started inviting sheep to London parties.

"Where are you?" Jess was suspicious.

"I expect you won't believe me, but I'm on an island with two demented sheep."

"I hate you, Nick. How could you go off to some lovely sunny island without me?"

"Wait up. Who said anything about sunny? Actually, this island is small, cold and very wet. And it's in the middle of your river, just down the road.

"Get someone down here to rescue me, quick. I don't fancy seeing the New Year in with just these sheep for company, somehow."

Jessica was torn between tears and laughter.

"We're on the way. Hold on."

"Not to this sheep, I won't. She's giving me a funny look as it is."

"Hurry, William. It's Nick."

"Nick who?"

"My Nick. He seems to be stranded with some of your sheep. Don't even ask." Jessica pulled William out of the house, not stopping for explanations.

"Your Nick, eh?" William Robb sighed theatrically and followed her into the storm. He somehow suspected that his chances of a midnight kiss had dramatically lessened.

The car's headlights picked out the scene. The sheep were huddled high up the field, as far from the swirling water as possible. And out on a spit of land, cut off by the rising level of the river, stood Nick and two anxious fat ewes. He was waving cheerfully, but Jess could see how real the danger was. At any moment he and the animals could be swept away.

If she lost him, Jess realised, there would be no balm strong enough to heal that hurt. How could she have thought there might be?

William was already swinging into action.

"Come on, Jess, there's not a second to spare."

THE sheep came first, kicking and bleating pitifully. "Good man." William Robb slapped Nick on the back as he emerged, drenched but still laughing, from the torrent. "I'd certainly have lost those two, and maybe the others, if you hadn't called."

"Darling Jess." Nick enfolded her in a very wet embrace. "Did you think I wasn't going to get here? I'd have made it in time if I hadn't spotted these two woolly brains in bother as I came along. I went gallantly to the rescue, then realised that I hadn't a clue how to get them back."

The rain cascaded around them, but neither Nick nor Jess noticed it as more than a slight distraction.

Nick kissed her.

"I've landed a job, presenting a morning chat show on local TV. I'll be based within commuting distance of the valley. We could easily stay here — when we're married, that is. Good place to raise that baby, don't you think?"

"Covered in mud, wet through, hair flat, accompanied by two pregnant sheep — this isn't quite how I imagined your proposal, Nick." Jess laughed.

His lips were warm when everything else was cold and wet. The two sheep grew tired of watching and waddled up the field to join their friends.

William listened to the bells ringing the New Year in on the car radio, and turned it up to let the others hear.

"Happy New Year, Jess," Nick said. "I just meant to surprise you with the good news. And to tell you how much I really love you."

"You definitely surprised me." Jess hugged Nick. "And I have a feeling that you always will." ■

BOB JACKSON leaned on the gate and pointed with his stick. "These fields used to be under water at this time of year," he said. "They were the river's flood plain before its course was altered. Now it just floods further downstream and does more damage. I could have told them that would happen."

Claire and Kirsty exchanged glances. They liked Bob, and Tip the dog, his constant companion. He didn't regard youngsters of their age as tearaways or nuisances. But it was half-past four, bitterly cold, and would soon be dark. They wanted to get home and knew that, once he got started on a subject, he was difficult to stop.

"Whenever there was a decent cold snap," he continued, "all of this would freeze over, and everyone would go skating. It was a marvellous sight. We had proper winters then."

Claire followed his gaze in the fading light and tried to imagine the smooth, swift movements of skaters gliding across the ice, their excited shouts ringing out in the crisp, clear air. It was hard to picture such a scene on the heavy clay fields stretching sullenly to the horizon. Judging from her frown, Kirsty felt the same.

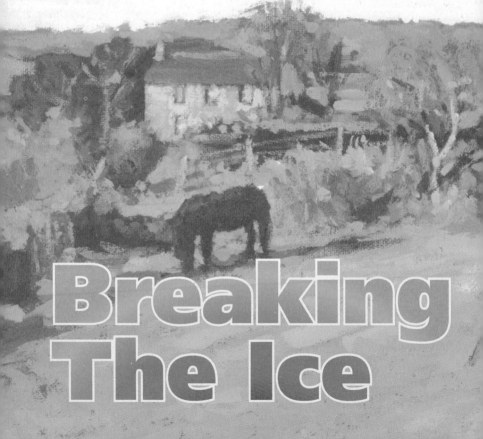

Breaking The Ice

She picked up her school bag, loaded with games kit and books from that day's lessons. This was the point where she and Kirsty always parted and headed off in their different directions. She bent down and gave Tip a farewell pat.

"I'd better go, Mr Jackson. My grandad will be wondering where I am."

Bob, who had been staring across the fields, deep in thought, seemed to wake up.

"What? Oh, yes, of course. Don't mind me. I'll rabbit on for hours, once I get going. Drives the wife mad. How is your grandfather? I've seen him out with that mutt of his, but never been close enough to speak. Has he settled in yet?"

Claire shrugged.

"Sort of."

"Like that, is it? Well, it must be hard, moving away when you've been in a place for so long. Still, there comes a point where you need to be near your family. Why don't you bring him round to my house for a cup of tea one day?"

Claire looked doubtful. Before she had started walking home with Kirsty, she had always been a little afraid of Bob, and still felt a bit shy with him even now. Even with his stick, he walked very straight and proud, and always

Illustration by David Axtell

by Rebecca
Holmes.

looked stern. When she had told Kirsty about it, her friend hadn't been able to stop laughing. She lived next door to Bob and had known him all her life.

And then there was Grandad. He wasn't the sort of person who took kindly to having his social life organised for him. How could a gawky twelve-year-old hope to succeed where others, including her parents, had failed?

Luckily, Bob seemed to understand.

"Oh, I see." He nodded. "Stubborn old so-and-so, is he? Well, the offer's open."

IT was growing darker by the minute. Claire quickened her step. She was glad Mum would be picking her up in the car afterwards. Lights were already on in most houses. The glow from behind curtained windows offered some comfort. Still, it was with a palpable sense of relief that she turned on to the short garden path and knocked on the door as she let herself in with her own key.

"Hi, Gramps," she called.

Inside, the bungalow was clean and warm. Smells of paint and fresh wallpaper still lingered faintly, mingling with furniture polish. The family had redecorated before her grandfather moved in — she had been allowed to paint the hallway — and today was the day Mrs Evans, the home help, came round.

Strains of Glenn Miller drifted from the lounge. Grandad was playing records on his old gramophone again. He had a compact disc player, but claimed it just wasn't the same. It didn't take him back, he said.

In a way, she knew what he meant. There was something evocative about his old records. They made her feel she had travelled back to a different era.

Claire thought of the collection of compact discs in her bedroom. They had been a sore point. In many ways she had enjoyed having her grandfather living with them while his bungalow was sorted out. She liked having someone who wasn't too busy to help her with her homework, and who had time to talk and put problems into perspective. But the walls in their house were thin, and he hated "that flipping racket", as he called it.

Although she tried to keep the volume down, sometimes it simply wasn't enough, and she wished the bungalow would hurry up and be ready so that he could move in. She was sure he often he felt the same. Somehow, it made her feel less guilty.

He was in his favourite chair by the gas fire, and raised his hand in greeting as she entered the room.

"Take the record off, there's a good girl. Save my legs."

Carefully, she lifted the arm and placed it in its resting position before sliding the switch along and watching, as if hypnotised, while the record gradually spun to a stop. A couple of weeks before, an antiques dealer had talked his way in and tried to buy the gramophone. Grandad's language that day had been a revelation.

"How was school?" he asked.

"Boring." She shrugged. Mum was always telling her off for shrugging. "How was your day?"

"So-so. Watched a quiz on the box. I don't know where they get some of those people. Most of them are hopeless."

"You should go on, Grandad. You'd make a fortune."

"There's a thought. Then that cleaner woman was trying to get me to join some kind of social club. I told her what I thought of that idea. You should have seen her face. Mind you, she gave back as good as she got. I suppose I'll be in her black books now."

"I'm sure she meant well." She could imagine Mrs Evans being suitably indignant . . . and enjoying every minute.

"Maybe. Your gran would have appreciated it. She liked a good gossip, but I never had any patience for that sort of thing."

Claire glanced at the wedding photograph on the mantelpiece. Grandad, tall as always but with more hair in those days, was in his Army uniform. Gran was in a simple wedding dress, clutching a modest bouquet in one hand while the other was slipped into the crook of her new husband's arm.

"I'll put the kettle on." Tea-making was one of her recently acquired skills, and the novelty hadn't yet worn off.

"There's a new packet of biscuits," her grandfather called after her as she headed for the kitchen. "Bring some through. I won't count how many you eat."

CLAIRE opened the pack of family assortment that had been left on the worktop and emptied some on to a plate. Mrs Evans was right in some ways, she reflected. It probably would do Grandad good to get out more, but not everyone liked the same things.

Whenever she walked past the community centre where the club was held, one glance through the windows was enough for her to know that it was just the sort of place he would hate.

Only the other day, Bob Jackson had made a caustic remark about it that had left Kirsty and herself in fits of giggles. Then they had started on another wave at the thought of what his wife, one of the club's staunchest members, would say if she heard him.

Still, Claire could vouch for the fact that getting to know new people made a huge difference. Take Kirsty, for instance. Although they had seen each other on the school bus, it was only when Claire had started taking the new route home to call in at the bungalow that the two girls had finally got talking.

They soon found that they both liked the same pop groups and television programmes, and both had pet hamsters which they kept in their bedrooms. And it was through Kirsty that Claire had come to know Bob.

She put the plate of biscuits and two mugs of freshly made tea on to a tray and went through to the lounge, taking up her now customary position kneeling on the hearth rug.

"Did you know that those fields at the bottom of the road used to flood and freeze over every winter?" she said. "People went skating on them."

"Did they, now?" Grandad polished off a custard cream. "A pond round our way used to freeze like that and everyone would dig their old ice-skates out of the backs of their wardrobes. Then some idiot tried walking across when the ice was too thin, nearly got themselves killed, and the council drained the pond and filled it in. Interfering busybodies."

Claire wondered whether a twelve-year-old had ever been called an interfering busybody before. But she knew what it was like to be bored. And it must be far worse for her grandfather, in a place where he hardly knew anyone.

It was now or never. She took a deep breath.

"Grandad," she said, "there's someone I think you'd like to meet."

He picked up his mug.

"Really?" he said, after a pause which Claire later told Kirsty felt as long as double maths on a Friday afternoon. "And who might that be? History teacher? Vicar? Some do-gooder?"

"Oh, no. No-one like that," she replied hastily. "It's Bob. He's the one who told me about the ice-skating."

She went on to explain about Bob Jackson. Although her grandfather didn't interrupt, he raised his eyebrows, which Claire suspected wasn't a good sign. But she had gone too far to back out, and pushed on to the end of her speech as quickly as she could.

"So you're very welcome to go round," she finished, a little breathlessly. "In fact, you'd probably be doing him a favour, because I'm sure he gets fed up sometimes," she added, with a flash of inspiration.

"You'd better drink your tea," Grandad said. "You'll wear yourself out, gabbling on like that."

Maybe Claire looked as crestfallen as she felt, because he suddenly smiled. His eyes, a clear blue which could be glacial when he was angry, started to twinkle.

"I thought your grandmother was the expert at talking people round. The boys won't stand a chance when you get to work on them in a couple of years."

"Grandad!"

22

He chuckled.

"All right. You make the arrangements, and I'll come along and be on my best behaviour. We can't have your friend being fed up, can we?"

THE following Saturday saw them ringing the doorbell at Bob's house. Claire's grandfather was wearing a martyred expression. She crossed her fingers behind her back, wondering if she had made a terrible mistake.

The door was opened almost immediately.

"You're just in time," Bob announced. "Another minute and a certain little madam would have guzzled the chocolate cake. Iris had a baking session this morning, and between you and me, her cakes are something special."

Claire shyly mumbled the necessary introductions and escaped to the lounge, where Kirsty was looking through some old photograph albums.

"Where's Bob's wife?"

"At the shops. She said if your grandad was anything like Bob, the thought of the two of them together was enough to drive anybody out. She won't be long, though. She wants to see what he's like."

Claire looked around the room. This was the first time she had ever been here. Bric-à-brac adorned every available surface, and the walls were covered with a profusion of paintings and family photographs. It felt homely and reassuring.

The two men came in. Judging from the constant rumble of their voices, they had found plenty to talk about.

Grandad was admiring a trophy.

"I got that for angling," Bob said proudly. "I've been a member of the local club for years. They have regular competitions, and the river's well stocked. Do you do any angling, George?"

"I should say so. Caught some fair old whoppers in my time."

The girls looked at each other. Clearly, Iris had been right.

Bob turned to them.

"Why don't you both pop next door for half an hour? I know for a fact that Kirsty wasted her money on a compact whatsit this morning, and I'm sure you'd rather deafen yourselves with that racket than listen to two old fogeys droning on. You can come back and stuff yourselves with cake afterwards."

They didn't need telling twice, especially after Claire glanced at her grandfather and received a wink in reply.

"Good," she heard Bob say once they were in the hall. "Now we can have a drop of brandy in our tea without them reporting us."

She closed the door behind them, happy in the satisfaction of a job well done. ■

A Blossoming Friendship

by Barbara Fox.

THE doorbell rang so early that I had to jump out of bed and answer it in my dressing-gown.

"Sue Marshall?" the delivery man asked. He was holding a bouquet of long-stemmed red roses.

"Yes," I answered in surprise. "Are those for me?"

"They sure are. Somebody loves you!" He winked as he handed them over.

I opened the little card clipped on to the wrapping. It read *To Sue, with love from Rick.*

The only Rick I could think of was the reprographics manager at work. Why would he be sending me flowers? Then I noticed that the card was heart shaped. One glance at the calendar confirmed it was Valentine's Day. What a lovely surprise!

In the six months I'd known Rick he hadn't hinted that he liked me. Even so, I was delighted with this gesture. I hadn't had a date for about eighteen months and it would be lovely to go out with someone nice.

There had been offers, but either they were from men I didn't fancy or from reps who came into work and were probably married.

Rick was different — tall, dark and good looking, with a pleasant but reserved manner. He was twenty-eight, unmarried and lived in one of the new flats on the other side of town.

My alarm clock startled me. It was time to get dressed. I arranged the roses in water and tried to focus on the day ahead. My fair hair fell loosely about my shoulders. It looked softer that way and I was running late.

"Have you been ploughing through your Valentine cards?" the receptionist asked as I walked through the door.

"No," I answered honestly.

The roses were a lovely secret between Rick and me. I buried my head in my work and waited. Surely Rick would pass through the office soon.

When should I thank him for the flowers? Perhaps I could follow him out so that no-one would hear. Would he ask me out today? My imagination was

Illustration by Bianchi.

working overtime.

It was so hard to concentrate that I couldn't wait any longer. I went to the Reprographics Unit on the pretence of getting a document copied urgently.

Rick was sitting at his desk. The background on his computer screen was a picture of beautiful flowers.

"That's lovely."

"It's Monet's Garden." He looked surprised to see me. "I like flowers; they

25

brighten up my day."

"Mine, too," I agreed, smiling.

"I could copy this on to your screen if you like," he offered.

"I would like — and thank you for the flowers."

I waited for him to say something, but he didn't. Perhaps it was because there were others in the office. On impulse, I decided to invite him to dinner. There was no time like the present. After all, it was Valentine's Day, and he had made the first move.

Leaning over, I whispered the invitation.

"By way of a thank you," I added.

He looked a bit puzzled but readily accepted.

"Are you sure your folks won't mind?"

"I have my own house, small but cosy," I said proudly, "and I like cooking."

It was all arranged as simply as that.

RICK arrived carrying a bottle of wine and a spray of pink carnations.

"More flowers!" I couldn't believe it. He was a real romantic. "You shouldn't have; sending roses was quite enough."

"Roses?" he repeated, looking puzzled. "Not guilty."

I laughed uneasily; he was teasing, surely.

He looked towards the vase.

"I'm afraid I can't take credit for those — unfortunately."

"Then who . . .? Look at the card."

"I agree it says 'Rick', but it wasn't

THIS pretty town twelve miles west of Inverness derives its name from the French *beau lieu*, or beautiful place.

French monks based at the Priory worked the lands in the 13th century, and it was visited by Mary, Queen of Scots, in 1562.

More recently the seat of Lord Lovat, chief of the Frasers, the present town was planned and laid out in 1840, with the town square holding the massive monument to the Lovat Scouts as well as the Mercat Cross.

Why not come to Beauly, and decide for yourself whether it was, indeed, well-named?

J. CAMPBELL KERR.

me, honestly. I only wish it was." He looked embarrassed.

"This is why you invited me, isn't it? I feel as though I'm here under false pretences."

"But I thanked you for the flowers at work!" I spluttered, my face turning crimson.

"I thought you meant the flowers on the computer," he apologised. "Do you want me to leave?"

"Of course not." I felt flustered. "I'm just confused. Besides, I've already cooked dinner."

"It smells wonderful. Should I open the wine?"

I nodded and he followed me into the kitchen to pour out two glasses.

Sipping the wine helped me to regain my composure. The meal was fine and we spent a pleasant evening chatting and getting to know each other. His main hobby was photography, and flowers, trees and birds fascinated him.

"You might like to see some of my work," he suggested modestly.

"I'd love to," I answered, suppressing the urge to add, "When?" and "How soon?"

"What did you think of my inviting you here?" I asked, realising that I must have seemed forward.

"Surprised, because you're sort of shy, but I couldn't believe my luck when you did." His warm brown eyes told me that he was sincere.

"Whoever the other Rick is he's really missed out." He gave me a quick peck on the cheek before leaving.

NEXT morning I awoke with several questions on my mind. Who on earth could this other Rick be? Who had sent the roses? Was it a joke? I quickly dismissed this idea, knowing that it would be a very expensive joke. No matter who had sent the flowers, they had done me a favour. They had helped me break the ice with my Rick. I was warming to the idea of "my Rick".

I arrived at work early. Jenny, a work experience girl standing in for the sales manager's secretary, was waiting by my desk. It was obvious she had been crying.

"Jenny!" I exclaimed. "What on earth's the matter?"

"It's about the roses," she faltered.

"You know who sent them?" I asked in surprise.

"Mr Brierley."

"Mr Brierley?" I was horrified. True, his name was Richard, but he was old enough to be my father.

"He just said, 'Send roses to Sue for Valentine's Day,' so I did." She fumbled with a screwed-up tissue. "I didn't know his wife was called Sue.

I'm sorry. He went mad when he found out what I'd done."

The mistake had been discovered that morning when Richard Brierley had phoned the florist to see what had happened to his wife's flowers. He had been furious with Jenny, and later he rang me to apologise for any embarrassment.

I wondered if my Rick had heard what had happened. During the morning I rang his number several times but there was no reply.

"Anyone seen Rick?" I queried, trying to sound casual.

"He isn't in today," came the reply.

I gasped, hoping it wasn't something he had eaten at my place.

After work I tried Rick's home number, but there was still no reply. I was desperate to find out how he was. Why hadn't he phoned me? Perhaps he was too ill to phone, or maybe he really was blaming my cooking. Last night I had had high hopes for this relationship, but now I wasn't so sure.

NEXT morning, the new background of Monet's Garden was on my computer, and within a few minutes, my phone rang. It was Rick.

"Are you feeling better?" I asked anxiously.

"Fine now, thanks," he replied. "It was a deep root filling and injections usually upset my system. I didn't ring you because I could hardly speak."

"You went to the dentist's?"

"I'm sorry, I meant to tell you that I wouldn't be at work, but I forgot."

After teabreak, Rick came into my office. His cheek was still quite swollen.

"You seemed so interested in Monet's Garden and the flowers we talked about the other night. How do you fancy this?"

He placed a sheet in front of me. It outlined the details of a weekend trip to Paris, including a visit to Monet's Garden.

My heart missed a beat.

"I've never been to Paris," I enthused, "but I've always wanted to go."

"Well, now's your chance." He grinned. "The photographic society is running this trip privately. If all the places are taken it's cheaper. My sister's going, too, so you could share with her."

"Sounds wonderful. When is it?" I pinched myself to see if I was dreaming.

"Not until June. So you've got plenty of time to get to know people. They're a friendly crowd. You'll like them."

We chatted for a while and I told him about Jenny's mistake with the flowers. His swollen cheek looked so painful as he fought against laughter!

"A dozen red roses, eh?" He pretended to look worried. "I'll have to make sure I maintain that standard next Valentine's Day."

I gazed up into his lovely brown eyes and smiled, saying nothing.

Standards? Paris, Monet's Garden, and talk of roses next Valentine's Day? I think we'll be just fine. ■

The Name Game

by Sue Moorcroft.

OUCH! Bless me, that smarts!" That's the gist of my greeting to the midwife! We've finally reached our local maternity unit after panicking through the rush-hour traffic, and I'm well and truly in labour.

And they don't call it "labour" for nothing, do they? Dear me, talk about hard work!

I grasp Pete violently. He winces, then pats my hand and turns to the midwife.

"It seems to be happening fairly quickly, even though it's our first baby!"

In no more time than it takes to swish along a corridor in a wheelchair we're closeted in a warm, safe delivery room and Pete's reeling off my details for the hospital records. And oh, isn't it boring? Doesn't it always happen? Pete gives my name and the midwife pauses.

"Pardon?" she says.

Do your kids a favour. Give them a decent name to start life with. It's not much to ask!

Don't indulge in clever name games — Minnie Carr, Orson Carte, Russell Sprout. It's not big and it's not clever. And please, don't — as my parents did — stray into "Boy Named Sue" territory. Because Mum and Dad, bless 'em, named me in memory of a much-loved, highly amusing and, frankly, dotty relative.

Uncle Des.

All right, they left off the word "uncle". But I wish they'd made some other consideration towards my gender; Desdemona's not bad, nor Desiree. But, perhaps from a misplaced idea of a trendy name like Georgy or Charly, my parents settled for Des.

I've never forgiven them. Des! More unfairly still, they christened my sister Elizabeth, a lovely name with a whole rainbow of affectionate shorts: Liz, Liza, Eliza, Beth, Betty. But me, I had to learn to cope with teachers unwilling to accept I

Illustration by
Amdi Thorsen.

really didn't have a *proper* name, or boys who didn't want to go out with a girl named Des.

The midwife bursts into giggles.

"It wouldn't be so bad if your surname wasn't O'Connor!"

CLENCHED all over by another contraction, I grimace as vilely as I can in her direction.

"Well, that's down to Pete! But be sure *we* won't give our child a really silly name!"

I waddle across to Pete and drape myself pitifully to have my back massaged.

"Our baby's going to have a fabulous name . . . Ouch!"

The midwife, no doubt quite used to being barked at by expectant mothers, grins.

"As I haven't heard of a baby called Ouch before — what have you actually chosen?"

Still in the clutch of the spasm, I begin to traipse up and down the room, dragging Pete along in case I need him. But, relief . . . it's passing. For a few blessed pain-free minutes, I can even smile.

"If it's a boy — James," I tell the midwife.

No matter how hard I try, I can find nothing objectionable in James, nor Jamie, Jim, or Jem.

"We haven't *quite* settled on a girl's name yet."

Pete laughs at this with slightly wild despair, knowing as he does that we've burnt midnight oil in pursuit of one. The midwife pats the bed, inviting me up.

"It's bound to be a girl then!" she predicts confidently.

"Oh, Pete, she's right, it's absolutely bound to be!" I groan.

"A little girl would be lovely, but we must have a name ready for her when she comes!"

*   *   *   *

It has been such a long day. Although labour raced along initially, it has settled into a calm rhythm of examinations, contractions and Pete manfully pacing alongside me ready for when I need someone's arm to pinch.

In between times, I worry over a girl's name, going over and over the ground we've covered a thousand times.

"Melissa? No, she'll be called Smelly. Belinda? That'll be shortened to Belly!"

"Paula?" Pete offers.

I grasp his shoulder in an unkind grip as another contraction grabs me.

"Her friends will call her Paul," I grind out.

Men! Honestly. It's all right for him, being born with an ordinary name.

"Ouch!" I shout.

I think it's time. Suddenly — we have lift off! Our baby's preparing to make its entrance into the world, and I'm still desperately testing names on Pete round the gas-and-air mask.

"Veronica? No — Ronnie. Grace? But what if she's not graceful?"

Then I shut up because suddenly I have to concentrate. I grip Pete's hand so hard the bones crunch, and listen to the midwife guiding me through this amazing, all-consuming, helter-skelter ride, her voice matter of fact and comforting.

But it's so difficult! I really don't think I can do this any more! Actually, perhaps I can.

In fact, I don't think I can stop!

A final heave, a cry . . .

CONGRATULATIONS, you've got a baby boy! Here he is!" the midwife croons.

Oh . . .! Look what I just did! I made a *son*, gorgeous in a damp and slippy sort of way. He's so beautiful I could cry.

"Look at his teeny-weeny starfish hands!" I sniffle.

"Have you ever seen toes that titchy? Pete, isn't he just wonderful?"

Pete is pink with emotion.

"Fantastic, Des! You were brilliant!"

And somehow, he manages to slide his arms round us both, kiss me and coo all kinds of meaningless drivel to the baby.

I gaze down at the tiny, slightly puzzled-looking brand-new human in my arms and wipe my eyes.

"Our son. We're so lucky!"

The baby yawns delicately.

I yawn inelegantly in return.

"Wow, I am *exhausted*."

"Can I hold him?" Pete asks.

"Of course."

Gingerly, he takes the baby from me and I really don't mind. I just want to slide down into a peaceful heap on the bed.

I manage to turn my head to look at my darling little boy with his dad.

"Our beautiful baby," I say drowsily.

I've never been so tired; I'm absolutely worn out from making the most gorgeous baby in the world. I must get some sleep.

"Hello, James O'Connor," I hear Pete croon.

I manage to hold out against my dreams for one last vital moment.

"Don't be silly, he doesn't look remotely like a James. We'll have to think of something else!" ■

"He's Not The Man I Married"

by Sally Wragg.

LIZZIE started off that great day, the day her husband came home from the Great War, in a state. She didn't even know whether to go and meet the train.

Patrick's letter had said he'd be on the 12.15 from Paddington, which would have reached Derby long since. Time enough for him to be home, so where was he?

She waited at the gate and watched the road, waiting, it seemed to her, for

34

life to start unfolding over again.

Really, she might as well be Lizzie Broxbourne instead of Lizzie Kilkenny. She didn't feel like a married woman, least of all Patrick's wife.

She couldn't argue with the fact they'd married hastily, and not at all as she'd always dreamed her wedding day would be!

Patrick had left for the Front almost at once, and she'd seen so little of him since.

He was so late Lizzie almost made up her mind to go inside. The sun beat down on her unprotected head and she was beginning to feel faint. Nerves, she supposed, wondering what they'd say to each other . . . What could they say, after all this time?

Suddenly, unbelievably, there he was, still in uniform, kit-bag slung over his shoulder, limping up the road, looking round as if he were lost. Perhaps he'd forgotten the house number — Patrick Kilkenny, who always knew exactly where he was going!

Strong, some would say obstinate, even, a man who never took any time to make up his mind.

He'd known at once he was going to marry Lizzie — he said he knew it the first time they met. It seemed to Lizzie now, in this heightened state of tension, that he'd merely pulled her along in his wake.

She couldn't help watching this new way he walked, though he'd told her the injury would get better with time.

"Lizzie — here you are then!"

35

He limped up to the gate, smiling a little wanly. Close up, it was a shock to realise he wasn't the Patrick she remembered. She should kiss him. Surely, if this marriage had been the right thing to do, she'd simply have run into his arms?

In the end, he saved them both the embarrassment and dropped a light kiss on her cheek.

"You're looking well!" She'd blurted out the first words that came into her head. He wasn't, so why say it? He'd lost weight, of course, in hospital for months.

She was trying to make him feel at ease, and the Patrick of old wouldn't have needed it. Somehow, instinctively, she realised this new Patrick did.

She opened the gate, and he came into the garden, looking up at the house. Her garden, her house . . . that was how it felt. Imagine feeling Patrick was an intruder!

WOULD she have married him if he hadn't shocked her into it by telling her he was joining up? They'd been carried along by a tidal wave of patriotism — everyone had, back in the autumn of 1914. At the time, marrying Patrick seemed like doing her bit.

They weren't the only ones — half of the staff at the Big House had joined up at once. People were snatching at happiness while they had the chance.

"Marry me, Lizzie!"

They'd been on the annual outing, to the seaside — one last bit of fun before the end of the world. It was a crazy day, she remembered, the sort of day you crammed a lifetime into, in case you didn't get another chance.

"But I don't know if I love you, Patrick . . ." She'd known she should be honest, at least. She felt something for him; she liked him, admired him even. She admired his force of mind, the way he always knew exactly what he wanted. He never hung about!

She was sorry he was going away — and to such a place. But how could he expect her to make up her mind so quick?

They were sitting on an upturned crate at the time, looking out to a blue and sparkly sea with white-capped waves. They always managed good weather for the staff treat — it was a standing joke, as if Lady Brockton ordered that, too, along with the food; a great ham, whatever you wanted to drink.

Mr Jones had already had too much. The sound of his deep baritone drifted up the beach: "Pale hands I loved beside the Shalima-har . . ."

Cook was splashing, barefoot, in the waves. There would be sore heads in the morning.

Patrick looked at Lizzie and smiled.

"I love you, Lizzie Broxbourne." He smiled. "Make an honest man of me!"

Patrick could always turn on the charm. In the ordinary way of things they hadn't done with courting yet and Patrick knew it.

Looking back, Lizzie could see how unfair all that pressure had been. What else could she have done but given in? She couldn't have slept at night if anything had happened after she'd turned him down.

"Come inside," she said. "I've made some tea."

He started to say he'd eaten on the train, but saw her face. He smiled then, trying to ease the tension, and mindful of the effort she must have made with the rations.

"I'm sure I can find a corner wants filling somewhere."

He propped his kit-bag in the corner and sat down while Lizzie mashed tea. Her heart was thumping, like the sound of all the sea all those years ago.

She'd always remember that sea, though she couldn't remember saying yes.

She did remember Patrick pulling her up, and everyone dancing round, clapping him across the back and shaking his hand. Mr Jones kissed her and said she was a bonnie lass and Patrick a lucky man . . .

Lizzie could feel his eyes on her shoulder-blades now. She was conscious of every breath he drew.

He'd had leave, of course, and his first leave had worried her; he was quieter, which Patrick never was.

Cook said it was the fighting that did it. Her brother had been out in South Africa.

IT got worse every time he came back, and after every leave Lizzie dreaded, and half expected, it would be the last.

She couldn't stand it when Mr Jones read bits out of the paper over breakfast, seeming to think she wanted to know all the danger Patrick would have to face.

But three or four months later, he'd turn up again — usually with no notice — thinner, paler, more than ever not himself. They'd just start to reacquaint themselves when he'd have to go again.

Putting the teapot into its woolly nest, Lizzie knew that of course they should never have married. They'd done it for every wrong reason, and they weren't the only ones!

Too late now. Now, they simply had to make the best of it.

She shivered as she remembered the day the telegram had come — Patrick was posted missing. At the time she was numbed, shocked, as if it was happening to someone else.

Was there, in a corner of her somewhere, a curious sense of relief? Not that he was missing — never that! But because of these doubts about their marriage?

"Never wed a soldier," Cook said.

Shortly after that, there was a postcard saying Private P. Kilkenny was receiving treatment for wounds in a military hospital in France. Mr Jones had to read that, because Lizzie's hands were shaking so much. Cook buried her face in her apron and cried, but Lizzie still couldn't feel anything.

Letters started to arrive after that. He wrote regularly, and she'd written back.

His shattered leg was getting better; Lord Brockton died; his widow sold the house, and Lizzie went into the factory.

He'd written back eagerly when she took on this place.

There was a lot of things she wanted to tell him, but rather thought she ought to keep to herself.

"What are you thinking about?" he asked.

SHE took his empty cup and poured more tea.

"I'm thinking how much we've changed."

How was she going to unravel this, to say how she felt, when she didn't understand it herself?

"It'd be odder if we hadn't changed," he said calmly, and drank his second cup thirstily. "You still make a great cuppa, girl."

A silence fell, an odd silence, as if neither could think of what to say. Perhaps there was too much to say.

"It's a nice house, Lizzie. Will you show me round?" He wanted to fill in the gap, she could tell.

She was only too pleased to have something to do. They got up and went round the house.

She'd taken it on a short-term lease, which showed how things had changed, that someone like Lizzie should even think of it.

Change was needed, right enough; people fetching and carrying for other folk — it wasn't right, that was what Mr Jones had said. He'd taken on a little shop in town — he'd always wanted to do that.

Lizzie had rented a room at Cook's new guest-house first, and then got the job at the factory.

When promotion followed, she'd found the house. She'd been so proud when she picked up the keys!

It wasn't that she'd forgotten Patrick; the way Lizzie saw it, she was just getting on with the rest of her life. Patrick had to have something to come back to and she was doing the best she could.

"I've been made up to supervisor . . . Did you get my letters telling you?"

"You've done well, Lizzie."

"What will you do yourself?"

Great-uncle's Farm

When dawn was just a streak of red,
The cockerel called us out of bed.
While city folk were still asleep,
We rounded up the straying sheep,
Fed pigs and hens, and milked the cows
Before we turned them out to browse.

Then breakfast — what a feast! Cold ham,
Hot buttered toast and home-made jam,
And tea from an enormous pot
Set on the hob to keep it hot.

A different world — and yet I find
Its highlights linger in my mind:
The copper, lit on washing-day,
And mangle, clattering away;
The spacious pantry — no deep freeze,
But milk in churns and home-made cheese;
The gentle giants that pulled the plough,
Ripe apples from the orchard bough,
Wild flowers that made the ditches gay,
And rustling stacks of new-mown hay.

And still the drowsy hum of bees
Or scent of blossom on the breeze
Recaptures for me, like a charm,
My visit to Great-uncle's farm!

— Brenda G. Macrow.

There, she'd blurted it out — Lizzie had always been straight to the point. But he had to do something. A groom or chauffeur with a weak leg would hardly be inundated with offers of work. And folk had got used to driving themselves, in a lot of cases.

They stood in the little downstairs parlour, looking out over the top end of the garden, and the flowers she'd planted days after she'd moved in. They were bright and cheerful — hollyhocks and red-hot pokers — they made the place her own. The rest of the garden was still tangled with weeds, but those flowers did look pretty.

"There was a man in the next hospital bed." Patrick sounded uncertain, as he had from the moment he arrived. He looked her straight in the eye, and took a deep breath.

"He's offered me a job, if I want it . . . He owns a garage, or he used to before this war. A thriving business, too, by all accounts. Cars are the future, Lizzie, and he needs help to get things up and going."

WHY was it so hard to tell her this news? It was good news, wasn't it? Many old soldiers didn't have as much. At least Patrick had a home to come back to, and now it sounded as if he'd fixed himself up with a job.

"His name's Matthew Cartwright," Patrick went on. "Lying there day after day . . . we helped each other through it, I suppose."

"That's good, isn't it? That he can give you a job, I mean."

Once, when he'd looked at her like that, her insides would have melted, and she'd have been putty in his hands. But it seemed there was more.

He took another deep breath. His eyes never left her face.

"The garage is in Surrey, Lizzie."

His words fell on her ear with the weight of a stone.

"Surrey?" How could he be thinking of Surrey when he'd only so recently arrived? His home was here, with her!

"I don't understand, Patrick. I thought you'd come back to stay?"

He reached for her hand and stroked it, a pleading look in his eyes.

"Matthew says there's a flat that only needs a lick of paint. It would be a fresh start, Lizzie, for us both."

That took time to sink in.

"But I don't want to go to Surrey, Patrick! Everything I want is here!"

"Matt really needs to know now, that's the thing. If I don't take him up on his offer, he'll have to find someone else . . ."

He wasn't even listening! Lizzie's heart sank. Moving was the very last thing she wanted, and it wasn't fair to expect it . . .

How could he suggest she leave everything she'd worked for?

Lizzie was getting angry now. He'd forced her hand once before, and now he was trying to make the same mistake!

"You don't even want to think it over?" He sounded bitter, not like himself.

"Oh, I'll think about it."

What else could she say? Her job, the house, this place, where her roots were sunk deep . . . How could she leave all that for a man she wasn't even sure she loved?

That thought brought with it a fresh, sharp pain, because how could she know whether she loved him, when they'd been so long apart?

"There's my job, Patrick. I'm doing so well . . ."

If only she could make him understand!

WHEN he turned away and began busying himself with the cups, Lizzie knew she had lost him. The little chance they had was slipping through her fingers. She'd seen it happen often, men coming home from this war, even older men . . .

The trenches changed them, and not for the better. They were restless, looking for something, anything, new.

"I'll unpack," he said flatly, and he took his bag and went upstairs. Lizzie stared out of the window at her flowers, tears pricking the backs of her eyes.

The day passed, and then another. Lizzie went to work, and Patrick tried to make himself at home, when both knew he wasn't at home.

He didn't mention Surrey again, and Lizzie was grateful for it. If he had, she hadn't a clue what she could have said.

"I'll be back around teatime." They'd just finished breakfast, and she was ready to go out.

"What are you going to do with yourself?" she asked curiously.

"Something . . . anything. I expect I'll find something to do!"

That was a flash of the old Patrick, and seeing it lifted Lizzie's heart momentarily. But then it was gone, and a cold, tired look came into his face.

He was a stranger most of the time. It seemed to Lizzie they were two strangers, thrown together and trying to make the best of it.

They'd have to make a go of it, because there wasn't anything else to do, but if being married meant trailing halfway across the country and giving up everything she'd ever worked for . . . !

Why did he have to do this now, when they hadn't even had a chance to get to know each other again? His lack of thought for her feelings annoyed her more than anything else.

But then, she reasoned, *he'd* given up everything; it wasn't his fault if, in the meantime, times had changed, and things had moved on — his wife most of all.

What else had he come back to, but her and this new job?

"Cat got your tongue, Lizzie Broxbourne?" Molly Hattersley finished her bacon sandwich and shut the lid on her butty tin. "Have I to drag it out of you? I thought at least you'd be happy now Patrick's back!"

She'd been longing to ask all morning, but Lizzie had been so quiet and unapproachable.

THEY were sitting on the little low wall overlooking the river, where they always ate lunch together. Molly might still be on the factory floor, but she didn't begrudge Lizzie her promotion; she took a pride in it, in fact.

"He's the offer of a job working in a garage in Surrey," Lizzie said baldly. As her friend's eyes widened, she filled Molly in on the details, only missing out how she was feeling about Patrick. She wasn't sure enough in her own mind to talk to anyone about that.

"Shall you go with him?" Molly asked at once, as if it was the most natural thing in the world that Lizzie should leave to live hundreds of miles away and not care a jot.

Lizzie watched a kingfisher dart, silvered blue, across the river. The rill plashed merrily over the stones, as if happy to be free from the factory at last.

Did she want to be free from the factory, too?

"How can I give up everything and go with him, Molly? Everything I have is here . . . I'm not the young girl Patrick Kilkenny once swept off her feet. Lizzie Broxbourne's grown up!"

"You married him for better or worse," Molly reminded her.

"Perhaps I shouldn't have married him."

The horror of what she'd said stopped her in her tracks.

Had it come to that? Was she really thinking that marrying Patrick had been the biggest mistake of her life?

"Should I have married him?" She looked at Molly, aghast, but how could she expect her friend to know the answer when she had no idea herself?

"You two need to talk," Molly said bluntly. "And the sooner, the better."

She was right, Lizzie acknowledged. They'd been skirting round each other since the moment he'd come back, afraid to speak their minds, afraid to say anything really. There was so much to thrash out . . .

Did she love him, for instance.

Somehow Lizzie got through the afternoon, half longing, half dreading the hooter. It went at last, sending the girls helter-skelter from their work. She gathered her things together and caught up with Molly, her footsteps dragging the nearer she got to home.

"You'll be all right," Molly encouraged her when they reached the gate, but

Waterford

S ET along a spectacular stretch of coastline, Waterford is the
gateway to some of Ireland's loveliest villages.

Although it's famous all over the world, of course, for its fabulous
crystal, Waterford's own varied history and wealth of treasures make
it well worth a visit.

J. CAMPBELL KERR.

Lizzie shook her head, opened it and went inside.

There was no sign of Patrick, only the remains of lunch on the table — the bread board and cheese dish, crumbs on a plate. Where had he got to?

Then she saw a movement through the window, and went outside.

He was in the garden. Lizzie's eyes widened in surprise — he'd dug her garden over!

The wilderness beyond her flowers had disappeared, miraculously replaced by tilled earth, rich and black.

Beyond, at the very bottom of the garden, a bonfire smoked, a wheelbarrow nearby, with a fork ready to pitch in the rest of the rubbish he'd unearthed.

How hard he must have worked!

He saw her and limped up the path.

"Well, Liz." He mopped his face and smiled at her, tentatively, but it was the old, winning smile.

"There was really no need," she cried.

"I needed to do something."

"You've done too much," she scolded.

He saw her looking at his leg, and frowned.

"It's not as bad as it seems."

She'd offended him — again. That was all too easy these days. She didn't know this man — she'd certainly never known him well enough to marry him.

But now too much time, too many things had passed; most of it not their fault. Patrick hadn't asked to go to war, after all, nor to be there for nigh on four horrible years before his wound.

HE was watching her face, her pain mirrored in his own. "I don't have to take this job, Lizzie," he said softly. "There'll be other jobs. I'll stay here and find something else."

She stared at him.

And when had he come to this conclusion? What had she said to make him change his mind?

The Patrick Lizzie remembered would have accepted the job and gone away. He'd have swept her along in his wake.

"But we haven't discussed it," she said blankly, as he shrugged. It seemed they were discussing it now.

"I can find work here, even if it's only digging gardens. There's always a demand for that, especially with food still so scarce."

"Your leg, Patrick?"

"My leg isn't as bad as you think. Honest, girl."

She thought of the months he'd spent incarcerated in a foreign hospital, in pain. He'd whiled away the hours talking to a fellow patient; they'd kept each other going, imagining what they'd do when finally they got out.

What else should he have done, how else could he have survived?

She looked up into his face — a little thinner than she remembered, but an honest face, and kind.

So what if she didn't know this new Patrick properly yet? There was nothing to stop her finding out.

After all, she could hardly have expected him to go through the whole blessed war, with all its hardships and traumas, and come out at the other end completely unchanged!

L IZZIE wasn't in the habit of spoiling other people's dreams. Somewhere, deep inside this stranger *was* the man she'd married, the man she was sure she'd have fallen in love with, if only they'd had more time.

"I know this is hard for you, Lizzie," he said, looking into her eyes. "You can hardly like me waltzing back into your life . . ."

"But you're wrong, Patrick!" In a sudden, dazzling burst of certainty, Lizzie knew he couldn't have been more wrong.

A light dawned in his eyes. He reached for her hand; his breath caught in his throat. There was something he wanted to say, and yet . . .

"Say it, Patrick."

"Marry me, then, Lizzie!"

"But we are married . . . What do you mean?"

He raised his eyebrows, and she understood.

"Oh, Patrick! That would be wonderful."

"We can do it properly this time round. I should never have rushed you, Lizzie — I should have taken all the time in the world. A little church, flowers, all our friends . . ."

Lizzie started to laugh.

"You'll have to get to know me first!"

"I know you already, Lizzie Broxbourne," he whispered softly. "I think I always have."

And suddenly she was in his arms, his lips on hers.

Her head was spinning too much to think. They still needed to talk. There was so much they'd need to do. Sub-letting this place, for one, moving, finding another job . . . Surely she could do just as well again somewhere else?

A tidal wave of joy welled up inside Lizzie. She'd started to say some of it, but his lips stilled hers.

Lizzie Broxbourne had come out into the garden that afternoon, but Lizzie Kilkenny ran joyfully inside, hand in hand with her husband. ■

Life With Louise

by Fiona North.

SOMETHING was most definitely wrong in my granddaughter's little world, I could tell. She'd hardly spoken a word on our morning walk to school. Louise and I had all sorts of conversations along the way — funny, sad, serious. But she was very rarely quiet.

I looked down fondly at her as we stood on the pavement, waiting for the lollipop man to let us cross the road. She was only nine, but already she had very decided views about her appearance. Her dark curly hair was cut into a short cap, and today she was wearing a vivid orange pinafore dress and a stripy T-shirt. There wasn't a frill or ribbon in sight, and absolutely no pink.

She had explained to me about pink when we were choosing the wool for her latest cardigan.

"Can I have red, please, Grandma?" she'd asked politely.

Pink was, apparently, too girly.

She looked up at me now, dark brows drawn together over her sapphire blue eyes.

"Grandma, you and Grandad were married, weren't you, before he died?"

"Of course we were, sweetheart." I took a firmer grip on her hand. "For nearly forty years."

She nodded, looking thoughtful.

"Did you have any boyfriends when you were married?"

"No. Just your grandad," I replied, beginning to feel slightly uneasy about where all this might be leading. Louise seldom asked pointless questions.

"Why not?"

"Er . . ."

To my relief, the lollipop man walked into

the middle of the road from the opposite pavement and stopped the traffic. I smiled gratefully at him as we passed, and to my surprise, Louise dimpled disarmingly. He smiled back.

"The lollipop man is Joe's grandad."

"Ah." That explained the dimpling, and possibly the questions.

Joe had been the topic of conversation on our walk to school yesterday. He was Louise's boyfriend, and they were planning to get married. Louise had lovingly pointed Joe out to me in the playground as the lad with the gappy smile and sticky-up hair.

As we walked down the hill towards the elderly red brick school, her preoccupation with my early love life continued. Had I been out with other boys before I knew Grandad, she wanted to know.

"One or two," I told her with a smile. "Then I met your grandad and we fell in love."

We were at the school gates now and she held her little face up to me for her goodbye kiss.

"Grandma, did you live with any of your boyfriends before you knew Grandad?" Her nose was almost touching mine.

"I most certainly did not!" I kissed her soundly on the cheek.

All the same, I couldn't help smiling a little as I walked back up the hill to catch the bus to my part-time job, trying to imagine just how Louise saw me.

I might have been a teenager at the beginning of the Sixties, but I had been a shy, reserved one, and like most youngsters, Bert and I had both lived quietly at home with our respective parents until the day we married.

I wondered if the lollipop man knew that his grandson and my granddaughter were unofficially betrothed. Better not to mention it, I decided, as I stood beside him, waiting to cross the road to my bus stop. So we just exchanged our usual remarks about how nice the weather was. Knowing children, the whole thing could be off by morning playtime.

Louise was subdued again when she came out of school. I waited, giving her time to tell me about it if she wanted to.

We'd reached the common before it all came out.

She still liked Joe, she explained earnestly, and she wasn't going to dump him, no matter what Emmie White said. The problem was, now she liked Liam as well.

"And *he* wants to marry me as well as Joe."

"Have they both asked you?" I said, my voice full of admiration.

"No, Grandma," she said patiently. "I asked *them* at dinner time. But Emmie White says I can't get married to two people at the same time and I think that's just stupid!" She went quiet again, and I didn't try to prompt her — I knew when I was about to walk into a minefield.

I noticed, though, that she stayed unusually withdrawn for the rest of the afternoon, so I decided that a word with Mum seemed to be in order.

*   *   *   *

"I know," my daughter-in-law, Helen, said, when she came to collect Louise later on. "She's driving me mad. I shouldn't worry — it's probably just a passing phase." She grinned. "Her dad says we should be grateful she's considering getting married at all."

"I hope you're right." I smiled. "I love my grandchildren dearly, but I don't do maths homework, enter into conversations about what age they should be allowed to get a tattoo — or answer Louise's difficult questions."

When I collected Louise from school the following afternoon she had something important to tell me. She'd decided that if she couldn't marry both Joe and Liam, then she wasn't going to marry either of them. It wouldn't be fair.

I breathed a quiet sigh of relief and said I thought it was nice of her to consider their feelings.

"I know." She nodded. "So I'm going to live with them both instead. Emmie White says you can live with as many boys as you want when you grow up."

Obviously pleased at having found a satisfactory solution to her difficulties, my budding new woman dimpled sweetly at the lollipop man as we crossed and ran off to pet my neighbour's friendly Labrador. I followed more slowly, wishing that Emmie White would be a little less free with her helpful advice.

It was good to see Louise smiling again, though. I watched her running ahead of me, confident and happy, with not a worry in the world. I was painfully aware of how quickly she was growing up and how precious this time with her was.

When we reached home I poured her some juice and made myself a cup of tea. Louise switched on her favourite TV programme and we settled down to enjoy our usual companionable half hour.

But . . .

"Gran? What did you say to Grandad when you asked him to go out with you?" she said casually.

"It was different when I was young, sweetheart. Girls didn't usually ask boys out in those days," I said.

"What did Grandad say to you then?"

"He said, 'Please may I have the next dance?'" I smiled, remembering that I'd been so frozen with shyness I could barely speak. "So we did, and it was beautiful. And later on he asked if he might walk me home."

"I asked my mum and she said she met my dad at a disco."

"I know, darling. Your daddy told me about it. He thought your mummy was lovely."

"Mummy said Daddy asked her if she was married and she said no." She scratched her head thoughtfully. "So Daddy said, 'Great. Get your coat then, you've clicked.'"

I decided to make myself another cup of tea. Philip hadn't told me that bit.

FRIDAY was my day off, so when the weather was good Louise and I left a little earlier so that we could take our time with our walk to school.

As we approached the common we were overtaken by two police officers riding the most beautifully groomed, gleaming chestnut horses. They clip-clopped loudly past us, noble heads proudly aloft, their riders sitting tall and straight. It was a lovely sight on that blue and golden morning.

We stood, hand in hand, and watched as horses and riders did a stately patrol along the length of the common. Then they crossed the road and disappeared in the direction of the park.

"Grandma!" Louise's face was alight. "Can I be a police lady and ride a horse when I grow up?" There was a trace of awe in her voice.

It was a serious question and I treated it with the respect it deserved.

"Louise, sweetheart." I put my arm around her. "When you grow up you can be almost anything you want."

Joe's grandad saw us approaching and held the traffic up for us. I puffed out my thanks as we crossed.

"You'd better run, Lou," I said, checking my watch. And she did, disappearing into the school yard before I was halfway down the hill.

The noise of the children's voices seemed louder than normal as I approached the playground, but nevertheless I was shocked when I realised why. Louise, Joe and another boy were in the middle of a very heated argument. They were surrounded by a crowd of noisy, excited children and I could see a lot of pushing and shoving going on.

"Excuse me!" The children broke ranks to allow me through. "Louise! Stop that, this instant!" I grasped her firmly by the arm. "Whatever are you thinking of!"

A young woman I recognised as Louise's class teacher arrived and, with great presence of mind, began to ring the bell she was holding. The children calmed down and began to line up, ready to go into school.

Louise, Joe and the other boy, who turned out to be Liam, were told to go and wait by the door, where she could see them. I decided it would be best if I stayed out of the way.

When the playground had cleared she walked over to the now quiet group and spoke to them. It looked like a very earnest conversation.

In the middle of it, Joe's grandad arrived, minus his lollipop gear.

"What were they doing?" Without his lollipop hat, his thick hair had a tendency to stick up like his grandson's.

*E*VER *since the first kail pot was hung over a peat fire, the Scots have had an ongoing love affair with hearty soups. From cock-a-leekie to partan bree, the list is endless. The most popular, often seen as a panacea for all ills, is the filling and comforting Scotch Broth.*

Scotch Broth

Put 1 lb lamb shanks into a pan and pour over 2 pts cold water. Season to taste and stir in half a lamb stock cube. Cover and simmer for 1½ hours, until meat is very tender. Lift out meat and leave to cool.

Put 1½ oz pearl barley into the liquid and bring back to the boil and simmer for 10 minutes. Dice a potato, carrot, celery stick, onion and leek. Add to pan and simmer for 15 minutes.

Dice meat and add to soup with 4 oz peas and some parsley. Adjust seasoning and serve.
Serves 4.

"Trying to flatten each other from the look of things."

"I'm really sorry. It's not like Joe to fight — especially with a lass." He looked stricken.

"To be honest, I didn't see what happened, and Louise isn't exactly a shrinking violet," I confessed.

TABLET is one of Scotland's oldest types of sweetie. An eighteenth century recipe was made by simply boiling two gills of water with a pound of sugar until it candied. By 1929, milk was being added, and today most recipes contain condensed milk.

Tablet

Put 4½ oz of fresh butter into a heavy-based saucepan. Melt over a low heat, then add 2¼ lb caster sugar, 10 fl oz full-fat milk and a pinch of salt. Bring mixture to the boil and simmer over a high heat for 8 to 10 minutes, stirring constantly. Add 7 oz condensed milk and simmer for 8 to 10 minutes, stirring often. Test by dropping a little of the mixture into a cup of cold water. It's ready if it forms a soft ball that you can pick up between your fingers.

Remove from heat and stir in 1 tsp vanilla extract. Beat with a wooden spoon for about 10 minutes, until mixture thickens. Pour into a buttered 9 x 13-in swiss roll tin. When almost cold, mark into squares. When completely cold, store in an airtight tin.

"So I believe." The corners of his mouth turned up and his honest grey eyes were surrounded by a network of laughter lines. "Our Joe talks a lot about your Louise. He tells me she's his girlfriend, but she's not into getting married."

"Sometimes she worries me."

"Her approach might have been a bit direct, I'll grant you. But our Joe's a bit on the shy side. I think he's pleased that a lass like Louise has taken a shine to him."

"They grow up so quickly nowadays."

"A bit too quickly if you ask me. I think they miss a lot."

I knew exactly what he meant. At Louise's age I hadn't had a thought beyond dolls and skipping ropes.

He told me his name was Joe, like his grandson.

"Maureen." We shook hands.

He didn't say much after that and I got the impression that Joe Senior was a bit on the shy side, too.

Louise's teacher dismissed the children, who filed into school looking decidedly subdued. Then she came over and spoke to us.

Apparently the argument had been about horses. Louise had run into the playground and announced excitedly that she was going to be a policewoman and have a horse when she grew up.

Liam had informed her that she couldn't because she didn't have anywhere to keep a horse. Her house only had a back yard and how, he had demanded to know, was she going to get a horse through the gate?

I was proud to hear that my granddaughter had stood her ground. She jolly well was going to have a police horse, she insisted — her grandma had told her that she could.

That was when Liam had said her grandma must be daft.

"By her own admission, Louise pushed Liam first. Then he pushed her back and Joe joined in and things got a bit out of hand. But there's no real harm done." She looked at me, brown eyes brimming with amusement. "I understand Louise intends to keep the horse in your front garden when it arrives. I just wondered if you knew?"

JOE SENIOR and I walked back across the playground together. The morning sun was gathering warmth.

"Do you think this means the understanding with our Joe is off?" he asked.

"Not necessarily," I said. "It looked to me as if he was going to her aid."

"I hope so." He smiled. "A policewoman in the family has got to be a good thing — especially one with a horse."

I couldn't help laughing.

"I don't know where she gets it from. Certainly not me — I wouldn't have said boo to a goose at her age."

"Where do any of them get it from? Times have changed from when we were young."

"Perhaps not all for the worse," I said thoughtfully, thinking about my loyal, courageous, outspoken little granddaughter, who could be almost anything she wanted when she grew up.

Joe and I reached the gate and stood in a little pool of silence.

"Can I offer you a lift?"

"No, really, I wouldn't want to take you out of your way."

"The only thing I'm planning to do is go home and make myself a strong cup of tea, to get over all the excitement. I'm on my own nowadays." He studied his shoes and I had a feeling he knew that I was, too.

It couldn't have been easy, telling me that, and I admired him for it. Joe was a nice man, I thought, and I liked him. I chewed the inside of my lip, wishing I had a bit more of my granddaughter's direct approach to life.

Then I straightened my shoulders. If Louise could propose to two lads in one day then surely I could invite a kind, decent man home for a cup of tea!

"Joe, if you wouldn't mind providing the lift I'd be pleased to provide the tea, with scones — home-made," I said.

His face lit up and the laughter lines crinkled around his eyes again.

He held the car door open for me.

"I don't know what your Louise would say if she knew about this," he said as he started the engine.

Get your coat, Grandma, you've clicked, I thought mischievously.

"It's probably best we don't ask," I said, and smiled quietly to myself. ∎

Tell It To The Bees

MARIA MURDISHAW had lived in Silver Birch Wood as long as anyone in the village could remember. I discovered her when I was still quite young, the day I wandered too far through the trees and came upon the old gypsy caravan.

"What do you want, child?" Her voice was low and gentle.

I stared at the elderly woman dressed in black, who sat on a fallen tree trunk whittling a piece of wood.

I'd heard of Maria from the whisperings of other children, who decided she must be a witch because she collected herbs and berries and had a huge black

by Barbara Povey.

cat. Some claimed that she was "away with the fairies" because she talked to her bees. But I saw nothing to fear in the old lady who sat so still and serene.

I told her I was looking for bluebells.

"I'll show you carpets of bluebells whose fragrance fills the air. But first you must promise not to pick the flowers. They're meant to live under the trees — they'll quickly fade and die if you take them from their home."

I could understand that reasoning — I knew that I'd be unhappy, too, if I was taken away from my home in the village. I agreed solemnly, and as Maria smiled at me, our friendship was born.

I was an inquisitive youngster, and adults were often too busy to answer my innumerable questions and satisfy my curiosity. Dad was always exhausted on his return from the fields each evening. Life was hard for farm workers — and the low wages meant Mam was for ever worried about making ends meet.

But Maria had time for me. She was never too busy.

She told me when the first cuckoo called in April, where the juiciest blackberries could be found in autumn, and how to stand as still as a statue as I watched the squirrels scurry down from their dreys, so that they thought I was part of the woodland and happily took titbits from my hand.

Maria taught me so much about nature — insects, birds and animals. She opened my eyes to another world.

I learned about her bees, too. The stories were true; Maria did talk to the bees. She told them everything of importance — matters of birth, death and marriage.

Maria was a constant fascination to me, and we became kindred spirits.

Moons waxed and waned, and eventually Mam learned of my visits to Silver Birch Wood.

"I don't like our Jenny hanging around there," I heard her complaining to Dad one evening as I washed the supper dishes in the scullery. "She'll end up as crazy as Maria Murdishaw!"

"Now, now, Ada, don't take on so. There's no harm in the old woman. She's lived alone for so long, it's made her a bit peculiar," he soothed. "Maria marches to a different drum than the rest of us, that's all."

"Well, I'm not happy about it," Mam snapped.

AS I left childhood and entered my teens, I must have become aware of the chaos of Maria's home, and the lack of cleanliness. But these things were of little consequence. Each hour in her company was golden.

Sometimes she painted translucent watercolours on scraps of paper — the first snowdrops, fragile as snowflakes, yet braving the cruel frosts of February, or a brilliant flash of a kingfisher seen through the weeping willows by the stream. These were things she thought important.

Though naïve in their execution, these pictures had an ethereal beauty, like the magic painting books whose colours emerge delicately when water is brushed over the pages.

My favourite was the picture of a cottage nestled in woodland — a cottage with roses round the door and, by the front porch, a cradle with just a glimpse of blue blanket.

"That was my dream," she told me when I asked where the cottage was.

It became my dream, too.

Over the years our village had seen many changes. It had once been an island amidst seas of waving corn and meadowland, but after World War II a regiment of council houses marched over the common and fake Tudor mansions crept ever nearer along the winding lanes. Farmland dwindled, and young people moved to the town to earn a living.

On leaving school I helped Mrs Dutton in the village shop-cum-post office. It wasn't much of a job, but I knew deep down that I wasn't cut out for a high flying career. My path in life would become clear to me in time. Meanwhile, I was content to wait, and my hours with Maria continued to be precious.

I became aware of rumours of a secret in Maria's past. There was talk of a baby born before society was ready for one-parent families. No-one knew what happened to the child, but Maria had withdrawn from public view to live her life with the birds and animals who didn't judge her.

She treated me with that same respect. With Maria I could always be myself, telling her my dreams and impossible goals. She levelled no criticism, never poured scorn on my ideas. I loved her philosophy of life.

"Live and let live," she would say as she carefully lifted a cockroach from the caravan floor to set it down in the woodland.

"That old caravan must be full of vermin," Mam said. But it wasn't. Even the flies, so often the plague of dwellers near woodland, were controlled by spiders which spun their silken nets in each nook and cranny.

✳   ✳   ✳   ✳

As I came to womanhood I began to "walk out", as we called it then, with Barney Gray. If he didn't entirely approve of my friendship with Maria, he didn't pressure me to end it.

Looking back, it seems strange that I never noticed any changes in Maria, nor imagined a time when I might lose my old friend. But I found her, one midsummer evening as the sun was setting, lying on the tufty grass in front of the beehives . . .

Had she been telling them she was about to leave?

The police arrived, and brought legal men to attend to the details. I offered to take care of the bees until it was decided what their fate might be.

My world was shattered by the death of my dear friend, and to add to my misery, shortly afterwards, Barney told me he had decided to move to the city, where there were more opportunities.

"Have you never thought of leaving the village?" he asked, his honest blue eyes gazing down into mine.

I suppose it was a proposal, of sorts. Barney was no good with words. But our relationship had not been romantic — *just good friends* would have been an apt cliché.

"No, Barney," I answered sadly. "My roots are here. I'll never leave." And I recalled Maria's warning about the bluebells.

I wished him well and promised to write with any news from the village.

"Like you'll tell the bees." He gave a wry smile.

I missed Barney. Not in the heart-rending way I missed Maria, but he had been a shoulder to lean on.

THE wheels of the law turned slowly, and it was spring before there was settlement of Maria's affairs.

Wild cherry blossom hung, delicate as a bridal veil, over the spot where Maria was buried. It had been her wish to remain for ever in her beloved wood.

Bright green birch leaves canopied the glade of bluebells and sunlight dappled my path as I made my way to the clearing, the solicitor's letter in my hand.

The caravan and its contents had been willed to me, together with the beehives and the ground they stood on. The rest of the woodland was left to Liam O'Malley, Maria's grandson, who had been traced to the Canadian backwoods and would be returning to England as soon as possible.

I sat down on the hummocky grass where Maria had died and told the bees what had happened.

*　　*　　*　　*

Several years have unravelled since that day. The gypsy caravan is no more, but in the woodland clearing, a log cabin has been built. A rambling rose climbs over the verandah, and in the shade stands a cradle with a glimpse of blue blanket.

I am pegging nappies on a line slung conveniently between two saplings when a slight rustle announces company.

A tall, weather-tanned man, his long unruly hair tied in a ponytail, moves towards me with the easy grace of a wild animal.

"Hello, wifeling!" he whispers, enfolding me in his strong muscular arms.

Then our lips meet in a long tender kiss and his dark intelligent eyes, dark as Maria's, gaze into mine with all the love and devotion I could desire. ■

A Dream Come True

by Ruth Walker.

Illustration by
Mark Viney.

I'M going on a cruise. It's been my dream since I was a child, when my Merchant Navy father held me spellbound with tales of voyages to exotic-sounding faraway places — Rio, Sydney, Suez.

It was impossible whilst my darling Ronald was alive; the mere mention of the sea was enough to turn him a delicate shade of green. We did once take the car across to France on the ferry, but it was a terrible ordeal for Ronald. So it was strictly packages by air for us, and when he became so ill and unable to travel far, we limited ourselves to long weekends in the country.

But now here I am on the quayside in Palma, waiting in line to board this beautiful, gleaming white ship. My stomach churns with excitement and my knees feel wobbly. A friendly officer in pristine white uniform examines my passport, then here I go, up the gangway into what is to be my floating hotel for the next couple of weeks.

I hesitate. Unfamiliar corridors and staircases, deep polished brasswork and gleaming mahogany, surround me. I suddenly panic and feel like an intruder. Who am I to think I belong in this privileged world?

A smiling steward rescues me and whisks me along to my cabin.

So here I am, in my own little space. Nothing too extravagant, but there is a picture window rather than a porthole, and the divan bed looks comfortable. All the furniture is ingeniously built in to make the best use of the space, and there's a tiny but beautifully fitted out shower room.

It doesn't take long to unpack. I travel light these days as I have no-one to help me with heavy suitcases, but I have brought along one long dress for the formal evenings.

I am suddenly filled with doubts. One's dreams have a habit of turning sour when finally realised. I wish I could be sure I'm doing the right thing. I'm not the most confident of people amongst strangers, and a woman on her own is often something of a misfit.

Still, I am here now, the cruise bought and paid for, so perhaps I should just hope for the best. This is my first holiday since Ronald died and I miss him so much.

It's hard not being one of a couple, and I have never found it easy to make friends on my own. But maybe I'll feel better once I find my way around and get my sea legs.

THE corridor outside my cabin stretches in both directions. Which way is fore and which is aft? I find a staircase and concentrate on climbing upwards, and eventually I find my way out on to the sundeck.

The sun dazzles me and the heat, after the air-conditioned comfort of the lower decks, hits like a hammer blow. Thank goodness I remembered to pack lots of sun cream.

The rows of sunbeds ranged neatly around the swimming pool look so inviting, but first I need to explore the rest of the ship. It's a bit like the first day at a new school – all the other passengers looking as lost as I feel, all strangers trying to find their way around this huge floating village.

Soon it's time to get ready for dinner. It's going to be a bit of an ordeal walking into that huge dining-room alone. I wonder what my table companions will be like?

I do hope they will be friendly people — cruising used to have the reputation of being a bit snobbish, didn't it? Hopefully times have changed and I will find a friend.

I hesitate at the restaurant entrance, and an impossibly good-looking young waiter shows me to my table. Starched white linen. Gleaming cutlery. Flowers. Impressive menus. And, thankfully, lovely people to talk to.

Jan and Chris are celebrating their silver wedding with this trip of a lifetime; elderly Doris and Arthur, who turn out to be veteran cruisers, regale us with endless accounts of other ships they have sailed on; and Sylvia, a lively, recently retired midwife, seems keen to join forces for some of the events and excursions.

And the food! I don't know how I'm going to be able to eat it all. Perhaps I'll do a bit of jogging round the deck.

I suddenly realise we have left port and are sailing out across the Mediterranean. A shiver of excitement runs through me as I realise we are at sea, and I am actually cruising!

SO now it's morning, after a blissful night literally rocked to sleep by the gentle motion of the ship. The sunshine tempts me up on deck for a stroll before breakfast.

I glance up at the bridge, high above me, and there's the captain with one of the other officers. He looks rather vulnerable with the responsibility he carries for the safety and comfort of all his passengers and crew. He notices me down on deck and gives a mock salute.

Breakfast over, I find a sun lounger in the shade, and Sylvia joins me. We take a dip in the sun-warmed water of the small pool. The movement of the ship causes waves. Now that's something we hadn't thought of!

We swap life histories: she tells me about her wonderful, satisfying years in the hospital maternity unit. Like many women in her profession, she never found time for marriage and a family of her own, but she seems to have found fulfilment in all the babies she brought into the world.

Sylvia is a lovely, warm, friendly woman, so easy to talk to, and I can see we are going to have fun sharing our experiences on this cruise — it's the first time for her, as well. By contrast my life as first an office secretary and then wife and mum seems very mundane.

She asks about my son, and if I will be seeing him over Christmas. I tell her that Alistair takes after his grandfather and will be working abroad, but that I will be spending some time with him beforehand.

The captain and first officer, deep in conversation, stroll past. Sylvia nudges me and points them out.

"Good-looking man, isn't he?" she whispers, glancing at the captain.

I have to agree. We'll be meeting him at the cocktail party tonight, and according to Doris and Arthur, who know about these things, we all get to have our photographs taken.

Now that will be interesting!

SIX o'clock in the evening and here I am in my cabin, all dressed up and staring at my unfamiliar reflection in the mirror. I can't remember the last time I wore a long dress.

When we were young, Ronald and I loved to dress up and go dancing. It's such a pity that nowadays casual clothes seem to be acceptable in practically every situation.

There's a gentle tap on my door, and here is Sylvia, come to collect me, dressed in classic black.

"Goodness, Mary!" she says in admiration. "Don't you look marvellous! That shade of blue really suits you. I wish I had been a little more adventurous."

We join the long line of chattering, excited travellers waiting to shake hands with the captain. At last it's our turn. Our names are announced, we shake hands, the captain smiles and says he hopes we have a good holiday.

We pose for the ship's photographer and then move on into the ballroom for a glass of champagne and delicious little canapés.

Sylvia and I are like a pair of excited teenagers, gazing wide-eyed at the luxurious surroundings. Shallow tiered seating fronts a dance floor with a small stage behind. We're looking forward to the entertainment here later in the week; Doris tells us we are in for a treat.

The captain makes a brief speech of welcome and introduces his senior officers. Then the small orchestra strikes up music for dancing. The officers move out to mix and mingle with the passengers, inviting the ladies travelling on their own to dance.

One or two couples take to the floor, and in no time the ballroom is a whirling mass of colour, the ladies' elegant gowns shown off to perfection by the black and white evening dress of their partners.

Sylvia nudges me.

"Look!" she hisses. "The captain's heading our way!"

He stops at our table — a tall, fair, handsome young man, smiling down at us. He holds out his hand to me.

"May I have the pleasure, madam?"

I get to my feet.

"Of course, darling, I'd be delighted!"

Sylvia gasps. My partner leads me on to the floor and sweeps me into his arms. I'm spun away into the swirling kaleidoscope of colour. I'm waltzing with the captain: Alistair, my son! ■

Young At Heart

They roam arm in arm across yellow-ribbed sands,
A couple now well on in years;
Holding pebbles and tiny pink shells in their hands,
With the ripple of waves in their ears.
As the sun shimmers softly above the sea haze,
The memories come flooding of earlier days.

While no-one is watching, the stockings are shed,
Their boots left to dry in the sun;
Paddling and splashing, the long years have fled,
For the couple enjoying some fun.
They rest by a breakwater, sorting out shells,
While the green waves roll in, and the sea softly swells.

Then, arm-in-arm again, homeward they stroll,
The decorum of age in their tread;
As dark purple shadows and evening mists roll,
Sandy shells on the table they spread;
They talk of life's joys in the oil lamp's soft glow,
And the years they have shared — while the firelight burns
*   low.*

— Maggie Smith.

FALLING FOR YOU

by Chris Firth.

RACHEL sat alone in the park, untouched by the beauty of nature around her, her thoughts miles away. Was it only four weeks since Paul had decided for them both that they should call it a day?

"Is — is there someone else?" she had asked, touching his hand tentatively.

He'd flinched, his chin jutting out.

"There's no-one else. I just think we're too young to be tied down. You'll thank me, one day!"

One month later, the memory of that evening still twisted inside — especially as it had taken only days for "no-one else" to materialise as a pretty blonde from their college. Since Paul lived in the same road as Rachel, she had to see them every day.

"But this is a big boat. I should sail it on the big lake!" A little boy's urgent plea strayed into Rachel's thoughts, nudging her back to the present, but she didn't look up.

She had been coming to the park every day after college, not just to avoid seeing Paul walking home with "no-one else", but because it was somewhere quiet. With an open book on her lap, she kept her head firmly down, chestnut tresses creating a curtain, protecting her from the outside world.

"The lake's too dangerous, Sam." The fatherly voice sounded close by. "It's this pond or your bath. You decide."

Rachel couldn't resist glancing at the child, his features pinched with concentration as if considering whether a small tantrum might help.

Clearly deciding not, he thrust his white boat into the murky water, then looked down again studiously.

"The lake's got ducks on." Rachel heard the child grumble.

"Good job we're here then," came the easy response. "They might think your boat's a nice, chunky loaf and start pecking it."

Rachel restrained a smile, taking the little boy's silence as confirmation that ponds weren't so bad after all.

"I wouldn't mind being four again." The male voice was now very close indeed. In fact, a glance told her that it was right next to her and belonged to a man not much older than herself.

Illustration by David Young.

"All you need is imagination and a bag of sweets," he continued, opening the latter. "Then a pond becomes an ocean and a boring uncle becomes a hero." He extended a hand. "Can I tempt you?"

Embarrassed, she shook her head.

"I don't mind if you pinch all the red ones," he invited, forcing her to look up.

"Thank you, but I'm not hungry."

"And you never take sweets from strangers?" His eyes widened. "Obviously, you're very wise. You must think I'm setting a bad example to Sam?"

Unsure what to say, she was grateful when Sam ran towards them.

"Uncle Stu! Why didn't you tell me we had sweets?"

"*We* don't," the man teased. "*I* do."

"It's not nice to not share," the child admonished.

Rachel couldn't help looking on as Sam carefully picked out all the red sweets.

"Thank you," he said politely and skipped back to the pond.

"That'll keep him quiet for a while." The uncle grinned. "I just can't keep up. He even talks in his sleep!"

"You look too young to be an uncle." The observation escaped without warning and something jarred — she didn't want to be stuck making conversation with a stranger. If she'd wanted to be tormented, she could be at home with two brothers who were allergic to silence.

"My sister's ten years older than me," the man explained, looking over at Sam.

Rachel could have mentioned the same age-gap between herself and her youngest brother, Luke, but she didn't want to offer encouragement. As it was, he didn't need any.

"Changing nappies at sixteen was character-building," he went on cheerfully. "Although I could probably have lived without the joy of potty training!"

He chanced the kind of smile that was hard not to respond to, but Rachel managed.

"Anyway, we're best buddies now — especially today."

RACHEL didn't want to know why. She wanted to leave, but she found herself trapped by soft brown eyes and couldn't help wondering why he was making so much effort to talk to her.

"You see, I saw you here yesterday," he went on, almost reading her mind, "but I figured that if I sat down and started chatting — 'Hi, I'm Stuart Cole, trainee manager' — you'd think I was strange. So I thought, if I brought Sam and you saw what a wonderful uncle I am, you might just speak to me."

His grin slipped as she stared back.

"As it is, you clearly think I'm very strange indeed!"

Watching his expression falter, Rachel felt a stir of sympathy.

"Not strange," she managed, "just a 'stranger'."

"In good company, there are no strangers, only people who've yet to become your friend."

"That's very profound."

"I'd love to impress you." One eyebrow tilted. "But it was a sign I read in a restaurant."

Almost risking a smile, Rachel dropped her head self-consciously.

"OK, you're an honest stranger, but I still don't know you."

"You've forgotten me already?" He feigned disbelief. "Stuart Cole," he prompted disarmingly, "trainee manager. Age twenty, living with parents, one sister — married with adorable son — one sixteen-year-old brother, best avoided unless wearing earplugs."

"Tell me about it!" Rachel could barely contain herself. "My twelve-year-old brother began his 'teen-fiend' training at ten and the other, barely seven, sees him as a perfect role model." She thought of the relentless noise and squabbles which drove her to sitting on park benches and sighed. "It's not easy being the eldest."

"My sister, Kate, used to feel the same way." His gentle gaze held hers. "Adam and I were horrors when she lived at home. Then she went to university and we were like puppies rushing to greet her every time she came back."

"My fiends," Rachel scoffed, "would be more likely to run in the opposite direction."

"You'd be surprised." He patted his chest. "Fiends have hearts, too."

Reminded of Paul's heartlessness, Rachel snapped her book shut.

"Well, you don't know my brothers," she said tautly. "But I'd best get home, just in case they're languishing without me."

"But you can't go," he urged. "I haven't guessed your name or pushed you on the swings!"

"Yeah!" Sam saved Rachel from a flustered response. "Let's go to the swings!" Boat under arm, he charged towards them and summoned his neediest eyes. "Please, Uncle Stu?"

The stranger, who no longer felt so strange, smiled patiently.

"OK, Captain, you win."

Cautiously, he turned to Rachel.

"I don't suppose you'd come with us?"

Endearingly, Sam held out his hand.

"Yeah, you can push me when Uncle Stu gets tired. I can't make my legs work properly yet," he explained intently, "so I have to be pushed a lot."

Reminded of times when she had pushed her own brothers on the swing, Rachel found herself catching the tiny hand.

"Well, OK." Collecting her book, she spoke quietly to his uncle. "It's Rachel, by the way. But no pushing me on the swings. I'd feel perfectly stupid."

IT was funny, though, because she didn't feel stupid at all being pushed by Stuart Cole. In fact, she felt quite lightheaded, soaring like a bird.

She even found herself spinning on the roundabout, shooting down the slide and laughing at her own weakness as she slipped from the rungs of a climbing frame, only to be caught by Stuart's arms, their faces so close that her heart fluttered. But the sparkle in his eyes forced her to step back, her head dropping.

"I really must go."

"Why do you hide behind your hair, Rachel," he asked softly, "when you have such a beautiful smile?"

Her cheeks flamed. Paul had never said she was beautiful. He had always made her feel that there were a million other prettier girls. Hiding felt safe.

She looked up apprehensively.

"Why have you been so nice to me, Stuart?"

"So you'll see me again," he chimed in.

Overwhelmed, Rachel's gaze tumbled. She had enjoyed their afternoon, but relationships weren't about smiles. They were huge, complicated jigsaws which she didn't have the right pieces to complete. So there was no point in trying.

"I understand," he added kindly. "You have a boyfriend."

"No!" Her head snapped up as the hurt inside resurfaced. "I don't have time. I'm far too busy with college and exams!"

He looked so stunned that she bit her lip.

"And I really have to go."

"But what if I never see you again? I'll be back at work next week, and I can't bring Sam to the park anyway. He's starting full-time school and Kate says he'll be too tired."

"Will not!" Sam insisted, abandoning the junior slide. "We can come every day." He faced Rachel, saucer-eyed. "And you'll come, too? You push me even higher than Uncle Stu. It's like I'm flying with invisible wings!" He flapped his arms.

She hesitated.

"Well, your mummy knows best. But if we do meet again, I'll push you really high, OK?"

His eager grin melted her heart, but as she looked at Stuart and saw his eyes shadow, she turned quickly back to Sam.

"Be a good boy for your teacher, won't you?"

The child nodded.

"I can write my name. She'll think I'm really clever."

"Definitely," she agreed, then caught Stuart's gaze. "Well, bye . . ."

Barm Brack

THE name is a corruption of the Irish "aran breac", meaning speckled bread. In the nineteenth century, pieces of baked loaf were dashed against the back of a house door to ward off evil.

Mix together 8 oz sultanas, 4 oz each of raisins and currants with 6 oz demerara sugar and ¼ pt hot tea. Leave mixture overnight.

The next day, add an egg and beat well. Stir in 8 oz Be-ro self-raising flour and pour into a 2-lb loaf tin. Bake at 325 deg. F., 170 deg. C., Gas Mark 3, for 1½ to 1¾ hours.

Makes 1 loaf.

Recipe courtesy of Be-ro.

"Well, bye then, Rachel." He offered her a tepid smile.

TWO months later, collecting her brother from school couldn't have been more inconvenient.

"But, Mum, I always go home with Anna on Thursdays."

But Mum wasn't bending.

"I'll drop you off at Anna's when I get back."

Knowing further protest was pointless, Rachel took solace in moaning to Anna all day. By three-thirty, she was prepared for the worst.

But she wasn't prepared for Stuart Cole.

"See, Sam's not the only clever one," he boasted. "I tracked down your brother's school and talked my sister into sending Sam here, just so I'd bump into you."

"You're . . . you're kidding, right?" Wary, her voice stumbled.

His eyes widened, then crinkled appealingly.

"Course I'm kidding! I had no idea. In fact, I'm only collecting Sam for two days because Kate's away and he's staying with us. He's been an angel."

"Really?" she said dryly. "Well, I'm only collecting Luke because I'm taking him to have his horns removed."

As Stuart laughed, Sam ran towards them, brandishing artwork.

"Look, Uncle Stu, I made a handprint!" Recognising Rachel, his face lit up. "Are we going to the park?"

Before Stuart could respond, Luke appeared, anxiously tugging his sister's arm.

"We've got to go," her brother urged. "I'm missing my favourite programme!"

"Sorry." Rachel smiled at Stuart. "One 'hornectomy' long overdue."

He smiled back.

"See you tomorrow?"

Already being bulldozed by her sibling, she simply nodded.

The next day, stunning her mother by offering to collect Luke, Rachel finished college early and swapped her trademark jeans for a long skirt. She even made an effort with her make-up.

Annoyingly, her hair was limper than usual and in desperation she piled it into a knot. Surprised by how much she liked the effect, she almost left it up, but somehow felt too nervous. Having thought about Stuart often over the last two months, she could hardly believe that fate was giving her a second chance. She didn't want to spoil it.

Fate, however, could be cruel.

"Mummy!" Hearing Sam's call, Rachel turned to see a beaming woman opening her arms to seal a loving embrace. She waited for Sam to notice her, but they strolled away, lost in conversation, leaving Rachel numb.

If the wonderful uncle Stu had cared about letting her down, he could have passed a message on through his sister, so he obviously didn't care at all.

It didn't matter, she told herself firmly. She had been here before and survived. This time it couldn't possibly matter or hurt as much. And yet it did. It mattered because Stuart had seemed so genuine. And it hurt because she had so badly wanted him to be all the things he seemed to be, everything Paul wasn't.

THE next afternoon, she found herself sitting on the park bench, huddled inside her coat. A solitary duck waddled past her feet and waded into the small pond, reminding her of one happy afternoon which she longed to forget. College students didn't ride on swings, they didn't make fools of themselves on climbing frames or laugh as they fell into the arms of beguiling strangers. They were old enough to know better.

"I wouldn't mind being a duck."

She recognised the voice but refused to look up.

"No worries about saying, or writing, the wrong thing." He paused. "And you absolutely never have to worry that someone special might never speak to you again." His voice lifted. "Unless, of course, quacking counts as talking, in which case that poor drake probably knows how I feel."

Rachel faced Stuart Cole.

"What are you talking about?"

"You didn't get my note, did you?" Dark eyebrows hitched.

"Note?"

"The one Sam gave to Luke explaining that Kate was rushing back to collect Sam herself."

Watching her expression register understanding, he smiled, relieved.

"I was worried I'd pushed things too far when you didn't turn up at the cinema last night, until I remembered where Kate finds most of Sam's notes."

"Bottom of the bag." Rachel half-smiled. "A week later."

"Exactly." Brown eyes danced. "So, after waiting an hour, I borrowed Dad's car, hoping I might find you here and that it was Luke who had messed up, not me."

"He's very reliable about being unreliable," she quipped, then sighed heavily.

"The film's showing again tonight," Stuart offered. "I could drive you home and pick you up around seven-thirty . . ?"

Five minutes later, they were parked outside her home. As she made to get out of the car, he took her hand, speaking tentatively.

"I'm glad you fell into my arms, Rachel."

"Me, too." She remembered her fall from the climbing frame, conscious of his touch, barely recognising her floaty voice.

His free hand shifted her hair away from her face, warm fingers making her neck tingle.

"You know, you should wear your hair up. It would show off your lovely complexion . . ."

Having tried the style only yesterday, she was taken by surprise. But when he misinterpreted her silence and leaned towards her, she drew back, wide-eyed.

"Rachel, I'm sorry." He paled visibly. "I was only going to kiss your cheek, honestly!"

"It's not that." To his relief, she laughed. "It's just that it's daylight, outside my home. I guarantee at least one brother will be peeping from behind a curtain."

"And you intend to disappoint him?" It was obviously a joke, but the tender smile playing on Stuart's lips drew her towards him and she found her mouth pressing against his. It was meant to be a peck, but she wasn't prepared for him kissing her back, or for the flurried feeling in her tummy that was different to anything she'd felt before.

Confused, she pulled away, but Stuart's voice was soft and low.

"We've still got a date tonight, haven't we?"

"Of course," she answered breathlessly and slipped out of the car, grateful to feel the ground beneath her feet as she waved goodbye. Even then, she didn't move, unable to quell the lingering sensation of their kiss, or the look in his eyes that told her he felt it, too.

And that was when she saw Paul, walking towards her with a new girlfriend. She saw his chin jut out and knew that was her cue to scuttle away. But not today.

"Paul!" She waved, absorbing his stunned expression. "You OK?"

"Fine," he responded uneasily. Then, with reluctance, he went on. "And you?"

"Fantastic, thank you."

"Great," he mumbled, desperate to escape. But Rachel hadn't finished.

"No, I really mean it, Paul."

"Really mean what?" he stalled.

"Thank you," she repeated emphatically and, with a broad smile, walked up her path, head held high. Closing the front door, she leaned against it, Cheshire Cat grin splitting her face.

"WHY are you grinning like a mad woman?" Luke was watching from the stairs.

"Because I am mad," she teased. "With you! Where's my note?"

"What note?" Nonchalant, he traipsed downstairs.

"The one Sam gave you yesterday, to give to me."

"Oh, that note." He pulled a face. "It's in my bag." She had expected an apology but he perched on the stairs, facing her accusingly. "How come you pushed Sam on the swings? You never push me and we've got a swing in the garden."

Surprised, she sat down beside him.

"I used to push you when you were Sam's age. But you got bigger." She smiled. "You got hooked on football and computer games."

"No. You got bigger and got all moody about exams and stuff." His eyes rolled disapprovingly.

"Sorry." Rachel swallowed a guilty lump. "But you'll understand, one day, when you're worrying about exams . . . and stuff."

"The swing was boring without you pushing me really high." He looked up, blue eyes wide. "You know, so high you're scared you might fall off."

"Good job I stopped then," she said casually. "I wouldn't want to scare you."

"Oh, no," Luke enthused. "I like that feeling — you're scared but it's a nice kind of scared."

Warmly, Rachel relived being pushed on the swing by Stuart and, unexpectedly, found herself matching that thrill to the sensation in her tummy when their lips had met . . . the same feeling she had now, just picturing his eyes.

And suddenly she understood. She was scared because these feelings were beyond anything she'd known before. But it was a nice scared, the kind that gave her heart invisible wings and told her this was her time to fly.

She jumped up.

"Race you to the swing."

"You'll push me?" Luke gasped. As Rachel nodded, he grinned cheekily. "Must be something in your boyfriend's kiss."

"Luke Taylor, you were peeping!"

"And you were doing it wrong." He sighed. "You're supposed to use your arms, too!" ■

All On A Summer's Day

by Kathleen
O'Farrell.

*Illustration by
Stephanie
Axtell.*

ALTHOUGH it was still early, sunshine streamed through the curtains, and in the tree house just outside the window, sparrows were chirruping in a joyous frenzy. What a perfect day it was going to be for the show, Jennifer Medway thought, as she stretched luxuriously!

She'd always enjoyed the Fenland

Counties Show, ever since her own childhood, and had bought the family ticket well in advance.

By her side, Jennifer's husband displayed markedly less enthusiasm.

"Do we have to go to the show?" Mike murmured sleepily. "It's the same every year, Jen, you know it is. And it's going to be one of those hot, tiring days."

"Oh, Mike!" Jennifer was aghast. "Of course we have to go! We can't disappoint the children. Besides, I did all that baking yesterday for the picnic.

"Now I'm going to get up and get cracking with the salads. We want to make an early start."

"I don't see why." Mike was still rather grumpy. "However early we go, we still get held up in all that dreadful traffic. Still, if you say so . . ." He sighed dramatically.

Mike, who'd always been one for family outings . . . who'd always taken such pleasure in the show. What could be wrong with him today, Jennifer wondered? Why was he so moody?

But perhaps he was just plain tired, she thought, as she slipped out of bed, and into the shower. Because Mike did work hard, and never refused overtime, always thinking of how the extra income would benefit his family.

It couldn't be anything serious, though, or he would have confided in her. That was why their marriage was so successful, because they never had secrets from one another.

BUT there was no time to brood. As Jennifer began packing the picnic basket, the boys could be heard rampaging down the stairs, boisterous as puppies.

Hard though it was on school days, she had no trouble with them on the day of the show. Johnny, eight, and Jamie, six, were downstairs and ready in no time, demanding breakfast, impatient to be off.

Leanne, at seventeen, was quite another matter, however. She only appeared, looking languid in pyjamas, when breakfast was almost over, shrugging her shoulders and saying she wasn't hungry anyway.

"Don't forget Toby, will you?" she said, with a glance at the picnic basket.

Toby, black and white, with gentle eyes, was Leanne's dog. At the mention of his name, he looked up from his basket in the corner, where he slept with Piglet, a scruffy old toy that had been Leanne's as a baby.

"As if I would!" Jennifer retorted indignantly. "I want us all to have a really lovely day."

"Of course," Leanne reminded them, sipping fruit juice, "it won't be the same this year, will it? Without Grandad Jim, I mean . . . dear old Grandad. How proud he was, being part of the show."

"Grandad Jim will still be there in spirit." Jennifer was determinedly cheerful, because nothing was going to spoil their family outing. Then, banishing sad thoughts, she became what the boys called "a real old bossy-boots", getting everyone organised, and seeing to last-minute practicalities.

Mike usually did this, she recalled, packing things into the car boot, but Mike wasn't much help today. He looked dispirited, and kept yawning.

COME to think of it, Leanne wasn't looking happy either, Jennifer reflected. Indeed she was nearly as morose as her dad. But there, teenage girls had their ups and downs, and it was best not to comment. Instead, she just remarked how lucky they were, with such a glorious day for their outing. But Leanne's face showed little interest.

It's all right for Mum, she thought bleakly. But little does she know . . . And if she dares to mention Adrian's name, or ask why he hasn't been around lately, I'll run out of the house screaming!

Until a couple of weeks before, when Leanne's heart had been broken, Adrian Walker had been the love of her life. Tall, black-haired, athletically lean, with twinkly dark eyes, Adrian had been the object of Leanne's adoration since their last year at school. Not that she'd got a look-in in those days. So many of her friends felt the same, she was merely one member of the Adrian Walker Admiration Society. But then, she'd never expected him to notice her, and was quite content to worship from afar.

It wasn't until they met up again, in the Fenland Building Society office where she worked, that the miracle had occurred. Adrian Walker, idol of Hereward Way Comprehensive, who'd come to work in the same office, had actually asked her out!

Leanne hadn't said much at home. It wasn't quite the thing to go on about affairs of the heart, so she'd hugged her lovely secret to herself — apart from a few words in Toby's ear, but then he wouldn't tell. But as far as Leanne was concerned, this was a dream come true, the love they wrote all the songs about.

Dizzy with delight, she'd gone to several discos with Adrian, once to the cinema, and once to the coast, on the back of his motorbike. True, there were often other young people around, mutual friends from school, but Leanne had always felt special, for she was Adrian's girl.

But then a girl called Arabella Wilson had joined their work team, and suddenly everything changed.

Arabella was tall and willowy and dramatic-looking, with the most beautiful hair Leanne had ever seen. Everyone was captivated by her, Adrian most of all, and before long he had transferred his affections.

"We'll still be good mates, won't we?" he said to Leanne, with that disarming smile, and all that Leanne could do was nod miserably, too proud to show her grief. As far as Adrian was concerned, it had only been a boy and girl friendship, of no real importance. Not love at all . . . How silly she had been!

Later on, when she felt better about it, she would confide in her mother, who'd listen sympathetically. And Jennifer would tell Leanne that every senior school had an Adrian, a good-looking lad, a teenage girl's dream.

It didn't do you any harm, Mum would explain, to cut your teeth on a teenage romance, or fall hopelessly in love with the school idol. Because, when it came to nothing, as it invariably did, you picked yourself up, and noticed other boys, the much nicer, more reliable ones.

Like Dad, Leanne would think. Good-looking in an unassuming way, with a quiet charm, and kind and sincere into the bargain. It gave her a nice, warm feeling to know that Mum and Dad were so close, so caring, and still had eyes only for each other. Not like some of her friends' parents . . .

MEANWHILE, Johnny and Jamie were hopping about, impatient. They were two jolly little boys, close enough in age to get along, and they loved any sort of day out, especially when all kinds of treats were forthcoming. They were first in the car, and on their best behaviour, when Leanne and Toby joined them.

"Good old Tobe," Johnny muttered, stroking the dog's head.

If the boys thought Leanne looked a bit miserable, they knew not to comment, so they just pulled faces at each other. When sisters were provoked, they sometimes burst into tears, and made you feel awful.

The Medways lived on the outskirts of town, in Fairview Road, where the little houses were all well kept and brightly painted, with neat front gardens. They had to cross town to reach the showground, and it would have been a pleasant drive, for the river ran through the town centre, fringed with willows, and rich with birdlife on its banks, but today they were soon caught up in the traffic. It came from all directions, from far and wide, for the Fenland Counties Summer Show was popular with both town and country folk alike. Especially on such a perfect day!

As they crawled along for the last mile or so Johnny and Jamie became tired of being good, and began to fidget, making cheeky remarks.

"Look, a tortoise overtook us!" Johnny cried, but to Jennifer's relief Mike just laughed.

"I'm doing my best," he said, "but you can always get out and walk."

And Jennifer thought, he's more like his old self already.

Not too much later they did reach the showground, and once they parked the car they immediately forgot the tedious journey, and fell under the spell of the music, the colour, the laughter, the fun-filled holiday atmosphere. Even Mike succumbed, his tiredness falling away.

Plockton

KNOWN as the jewel of the Highlands, Plockton retains its village charms despite being one of the most popular and photogenic places in Scotland.

Its proximity to the Gulf Stream and sheltered natural harbour provide ideal conditions for the palm trees and subtropical flowers which abound.

Fans of the TV series "Hamish Macbeth" will find themselves in familiar territory — the programme was filmed here in Plockton.

J. CAMPBELL KERR.

For Jennifer, the huge marquee full of flowers and plants was the main attraction, where local growers exhibited their most beautiful specimens, and she gazed at them all lovingly.

But then, Jennifer had always adored flowers. She had been working in a florist's shop when she first met Michael Medway, and often smiled to herself at the recollection. It must have been the one and only time in his life that Mike had been openly flirtatious — quiet, decorous, dear old Mike.

"My word," he'd cried in admiration, looking at the slender girl in the pale green overall, with her white skin and smooth golden hair, "they've certainly matched the young lady to the job! I bet your name is Lily!"

"No, it's Jennifer," she'd answered, laughing off the compliment.

After that, Michael Medway had bought a lot of flowers, yet he'd never been flirty with Jennifer again, always treating her with respect, and a little awe. Until one day, when he plucked up courage to invite her to his firm's Christmas dinner-dance . . . and she had accepted.

It had been far and away the most wonderful evening of Mike's life, and by the time it was over he and Jennifer had both known they were meant for each other.

"ISN'T this glorious?" Jennifer's eyes were shining, as she gazed around her. "Even if it does make one's own little garden seem like a window-box! Oh, Mike, I could stay in here all day!"

But Mike liked seeing the animals, too, and so did Johnny and Jamie, while Leanne had always longed for a pony, so they went to the section where Fenland farmers proudly exhibited their livestock.

After they'd been to the Food Hall, full of speciality cheeses, butter and cream, and gorgeous, scrumptious cakes, and dairy ices, they found they wanted to go in different directions.

"That's all right," Jennifer agreed, "as long as we meet up by the clock tower for lunch. One o'clock, remember!"

She didn't mind a bit. But she made sure the boys were never out of her sight . . .

Leanne, so taken up with her own sad-sweet thoughts, felt it was a good idea to be alone, so she wandered off — with Toby.

Although her spirits had risen somewhat, there was still that little ache inside her, that emptiness, that wouldn't go away. She couldn't stop thinking about Adrian, yet didn't really want to . . . fickle Adrian, who had seemed to be growing so fond of her, but had then rejected her, in such a casual way. And she felt so lonely. Even after just a few weeks together, you could miss someone dreadfully. And she still missed Grandad Jim, though in a different sort of way.

It was at times like this that she longed for Grandad Jim still to be around.

Mum's father, known to his friends as Jolly Jim Jarvis, had been an important part of the show for many a year — but never would be again. He'd slipped away from this world, quietly, suddenly, the previous autumn, and they all missed his warmth, his laughter, his unfailing optimism.

Now Leanne spent her free time taking Toby for walks. His devotion, at least, was unchanging. You're my Special Girl, his soulful eyes seemed to say, whenever he looked up at her. Dear, loyal Toby.

Despite her misery, Leanne enjoyed herself much more than she had expected, as she meandered along in the sunshine, gazing at stalls of every kind. But the craft stalls she found particularly fascinating. What patience some people had!

Leanne, a very modern girl indeed, who thought needlework fiddly and boring, found it almost incredible that there were still people around — gifted people, of course — who could sit for hours, working away meticulously on embroidery, or delicate lace, or intricate patchwork that glowed in rich, beautiful colours like a stained-glass window.

Just after she'd discovered a lovely stall displaying pretty china, and had chosen a charming plate, hand-painted with flowers, for her mother's birthday, Leanne heard her name called. She turned in surprise, and saw that a pleasant-looking lady was beckoning to her.

The lady was standing behind a stall with a purple banner above it, spelling out the words *Horse And Pony Haven* in big white letters, and as she moved towards her, Leanne remembered her vaguely. She'd once lived in Fairview Road, but what was her name?

YOU'RE Leanne Medway, aren't you?" The lady looked pleased to see her. "And can this be Toby? If so, I remember him as a puppy. You got him for your birthday, when you were a little girl."

And suddenly Leanne recalled the Halfacre family, who'd lived a few doors up. There had been a boy called Harry, a skinny lad, long-legged and freckled, who'd sometimes played with her. Nice people, but they'd moved away when Leanne was still quite young.

It was lovely to meet up with old friends again, and there was so much to talk about. Mrs Halfacre found Leanne a stool and they settled down to a lengthy chat, with Toby curled up patiently at Leanne's feet in silent approval. He was very relieved to see his Special Girl look so much brighter.

There were all kinds of items for sale on the stall, all bearing irresistible pictures of horses and ponies — donkeys, too — with the Haven logo on, and Mrs Halfacre had to keep stopping in order to serve her customers, but even so, Leanne hadn't enjoyed herself as much for weeks.

After being left a large old property out in the fens, the Halfacres had worked tirelessly to achieve their ambition of setting up a sanctuary for unwanted or ill-used horses and ponies.

As she listened to Mrs Halfacre's tales, some heart-rending, some so full of humour, Leanne was torn between laughter and tears.

"If only I could help!" she cried. "If only there was something I could do!"

"But there is, Leanne, dear." Marion Halfacre wasn't going to let this golden opportunity slip by. "You'd be more than welcome to join our team of voluntary helpers. We've several young people, teenagers like yourself, who help out in their free time. Saturdays mostly . . . All horse and pony mad, of course."

"There's something about ponies." Leanne sighed. "When I was little, and had a wish, it was always for a pony — though how it would have fitted into our back garden, I don't know." And they both laughed.

Then Leanne remembered to enquire after Harry.

"Why, Harry's doing fine," his mother assured her. "He's studying to be a vet — he'll be a great help to us when he qualifies. But he always lends a hand when he's home from college. In fact, he'll be joining me very soon . . .

"Oh, Leanne, do wait a few minutes more," she went on, for she'd seen Leanne glance at her watch. "Harry would be most upset if he missed seeing you . . . Why, I do believe this is him now!"

Leanne jumped up. She stood there, rooted in delightful disbelief.

COULD this really be the boy she'd played "house" with, under the hawthorn hedge, with a doll's tea-set and a bag of jelly babies? He certainly wouldn't fit under a hedge now . . .

Harry had grown very tall, but he was still lean, and still freckled, and Leanne would easily have recognised him — that endearing grin, the nice grey eyes, the rather floppy brown hair; even the way he walked was familiar. And it was wonderful, meeting him again. There was no constraint or awkwardness, just a pleasant feeling of friendship renewed.

"If you really want to come and help on a Saturday," Harry said, "I can arrange a lift for you. And yes, you may bring Toby. It's not every girl's idea of fun, of course, but it has its perks. Some of our horses need to be exercised, which means riding them. Did you ever learn to ride, Leanne?"

"Oh, no!" Leanne shook her head. "The only ponies I ever knew were in story-books. I just dreamed about them . . . and stuck pictures of them around my bedroom walls."

"Well, then," Harry said, in his kind, sensible way, "I'll just have to teach you, won't I? It's not all that difficult . . ."

He looked quite dismayed when Leanne, sparkly-eyed and nearly dizzy with excitement, said she had to go.

"I'm meeting up with the family for lunch," she cried guiltily, "and I'm

Pedal Power

With a wave of the hand and an elegant air,
We cycle along as the good townsfolk stare;
On quiet country lanes we are tempted to race,
Feeling fresh breezes cool the hot sun on each face.

Where sweet honeysuckle and wild roses bloom,
The valleys are green, and some steep hillsides loom,
There are cows in the meadows and lambs by a stream —
And our wonderful tour passes on like a dream.

Good folk move aside as we follow the track,
But with so much to see we are loth to turn back.
We drink from a sweet sparkling spring by the way,
Where a village rest tempts us — and hear a man say:
"This new-fangled nonsense will surely not last!
Such contraptions will soon be a whim of the past!"
— *Maggie Smith.*

going to be late. But you know where to find me — still at the same address!"

With hurried goodbyes to Harry and his mother, Leanne and Toby set off for the clock tower.

And Harry Halfacre watched her until she was out of sight, a small half-smile on his face.

The others were already there by the time Leanne and Toby arrived, and Mum was setting out the picnic. They all had terrific appetites, even Leanne, who suddenly realised how happy and relaxed she was feeling . . . better than she'd felt for ages.

"Guess who I've just been talking to?" she said to Mum and Dad, and they were both delighted to hear the news of the Halfacre family. And they were pleased, too, at seeing Leanne look so animated, her old self again.

But what were the two little boys talking about so earnestly? They didn't remember the Halfacres, but they were caught up in memories of their own, precious memories of Grandad Jim. They had both been so fond of him, and still missed him very much.

He'd been their baby-sitter from their earliest days, and his great joy was to read to them from an old and treasured book of fairytales. It had a pretty cottage on the cover, with a big white bird perched on the roof — a stork, he told them.

Johnny and Jamie had really loved those stories, so far removed from everyday life, and read in Grandad's rich country voice.

B UT it was late afternoon when they all missed Grandad Jim the most, when they sat on the grass in the corner of the showground, and listened to the band. Because Jolly Jim Jarvis should have been there — a darling, twinkly-eyed, tubby little man, blowing his trumpet for all he was worth. He'd been so proud to be a bandsman, and was held in such high regard and affection by all who knew him.

As they listened to the rousing music, Jennifer's eyes filled with tears.

"This was his favourite Sousa march," she murmured, and Mike's arm went around her shoulders, his cheek pressed against hers in silent sympathy.

The little boys were feeling wistful, too. Sometimes Grandad Jim had winked at them as he played, and though they thought it was a bit daring — like winking in church — it made them feel special. If only he could wink at them again, just once more!

"Do you think Grandad Jim still remembers us?" Jamie asked, and his big brother Johnny was quick to reassure him.

"Of course he does, silly. Because we were his little scallywags, weren't we?"

Johnny wasn't sure what scallywags were, but Grandad Jim always called them that when he hugged them.

Secretly, though, Johnny wished they could have a sign — just a tiny little sign would do — that Grandad Jim and his fairytale world had not gone for ever.

✳   ✳   ✳   ✳

It had been a great day out, and driving home, they all felt the benefit of it.

"I'm sorry I was such a grouchy old bear this morning, Jen," Mike apologised. "The truth is I was just feeling drained. Perhaps I should cut down on the overtime a bit."

"I do wish you would." Jennifer was delighted. "For a while, anyway. It's a waste of lovely summer evenings when you're not at home to share them with me." A dreamy contentment swept over her at the prospect of lazy summer evenings in the garden with Mike. Then, as they turned into Fairview Road, a shout went up from the little boys.

"Look! Just look at our house!" they cried excitedly.

They stared, at a loss for words. For there, perched on their roof, was a big white bird with a long neck, long skinny legs, and a long yellow beak. It had little, bright, piercing eyes that darted everywhere, and big feet that were flat and star-shaped. Why, it might well have flown off the cover of Grandad Jim's fairytale book! No wonder Johnny and Jamie took it to be a stork . . .

Their parents knew better. It wasn't a stork, but a heron from the riverbank who'd flown in on a foraging expedition, looking for fish-ponds. But what a happy coincidence that it had come that day! Not for anything would they shatter their small sons' illusions that it was, in some magical way, connected with their beloved grandfather.

"Do you think it's brought us a baby?" Jamie cried hopefully, and they were all laughing so much as they surged through the door that they would all remember this particular day for a long time to come.

✳   ✳   ✳   ✳

A while later, when the house was still and quiet, with all the tired folk in their beds, Toby snuggled down in his basket in the kitchen, comfortably full after his favourite chicken supper. His old tartan blanket with holes in it had a nice, familiar, doggy smell, and Piglet was beside him.

I did well today, Toby thought — no wonder I'm dog-tired! For I never took my eyes off my Special Girl, the best girl ever. But it was a good day, a very satisfactory day, and my Special Girl came back a lot happier than she went. What was it she whispered in my ear, when she said goodnight?

"No more lonely Saturdays, Tobe. We're going to have such fun!"

Then Toby, well content, shut his eyes, and with a little snort and a snuffle, fell asleep. All was well with his small world, and the excitement of the Fenland Counties Show was over — for another year! ▪

THE prom is crowded on this, the first sunny Saturday of the year. I gaze towards the grey-green sea, then slip my hand into my jacket pocket and touch the letter from Carl. I practically know it off by heart.

I hope your mother will post this on to you, wherever you are. I love you, Lois. Please come back . . . we can talk at Stuart's wedding . . .

I withdraw my hand and sigh. Talk! What's the point? We only end up arguing.

I shiver, in spite of the sun. Carl always called our many rows just "healthy disagreements", seeming to thrive on them. I hate rows.

"Opposites, you two," my mother declared, on first meeting Carl.

And she was right — Carl loves parties, crowds; I try to avoid them. And then there's our different tastes in music, films, TV programmes . . . you name it.

But I can't forget, either, the joy and laughter we've shared — all those wonderful rainbows in between the showers.

I take out a tissue and blow my nose, then tell myself not to be so pathetic. I was the one to end the engagement and move two hundred miles away to this seaside town to start a new life, wasn't I? So why don't I get on and do just that?

I don't have to go back for Stuart's wedding. He's Carl's friend, after all, not mine.

Looking at all these happy families enjoying themselves on the beach, I suddenly feel so alone. What will Carl be doing now? I really miss our long rambles, the pub lunches — everything. When you walk away from someone, you also walk away from a way of life . . .

Stop this, Lois, I tell myself firmly. Be positive. The sun is shining, you've a good job, a nice flat and a whole new future ahead of you!

Ahead, I see a small queue for ice-cream and I hurry towards it. A delicious way to console myself . . .

The woman in front of me, harassed by a couple of children, turns away, balancing three cones. A boy of around eight jumps up to grab one of them.

"Watch it, Craig!" she yells. Too late; in seconds the ground in front of her is a puddle of whipped ice-cream, peppered with bits of broken cone.

"I didn't mean to!" the lad insists, looking horrified.

The younger boy begins to cry

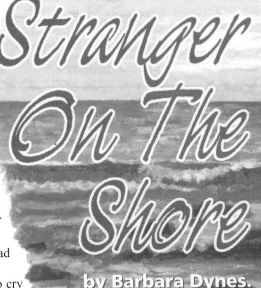

Stranger On The Shore

by Barbara Dynes.

82

and their poor mother looks exhausted. In my present emotional state, this is all I need. Act, Lois, before you burst into tears . . . I grin at the salesman, ask the family to wait and buy four cornets.

"Oh, how kind — you don't have to . . ." the mother begins.

"Oh, but I do!" I hand out the ice-cream. The boys' faces are a study as they thank me.

"Can't stand the noise, you see!" I add, with a grin.

"Well, thanks. That was really nice of you." She smiles. "You on your own?" I nod.

"I'm Sally," she says. "Come and join us on the beach!"

WHY not, I think, as I introduce myself. A family afternoon . . . not exactly me, but then I have to get used to a new me.

"It's quieter at this end of the beach, isn't it?" Sally asks, as we all sit down.

I wriggle out of my sandals. The sand feels pleasantly warm and gritty on my bare feet.

"I wouldn't know," I answer, trying to catch the drips of ice-cream around the cone.

"I'm a stranger — I've only been here a month or so."

"Oh, I see." Sally smiles. "Andy, watch that ice-cream!"

Andy, absently licking away, doesn't look up from his book.

"The quiet one," Sally explains. "Can't get enough of Harry Potter!"

Craig, the older boy, finishes his cornet then picks up his spade and begins to dig vigorously, his face bright red, hair sticking up like a brush. I smile. That hole is so important to Craig.

How nice to be a child again, to live for the moment, with no big emotional decisions to make . . . Suddenly, sand showers over Andy and, to a lesser extent, over Sally and me.

"Craig! I won't tell you again!" Sally shouts.

Illustration by David Young.

83

Andy flings down his book and charges at his brother who, kicking up more sand, runs towards the sea.

Andy races after him.

"Children!" Sally sighs. "Who'd have them?"

I smile wistfully. I would. Two, Carl and I planned . . . I look away.

"Have you made many friends at work?" Sally asks.

I think about my new job in a massive, open-plan accounts office of a busy computer firm.

"No, not really," I answer.

Sally stands up, shielding her eyes from the sun as she searches the beach.

"Give it time, Lois," she says sympathetically. "It's never easy to begin with."

I bite my lip. I've been too occupied with my own feelings about Carl to get really involved with anything or anyone. Have I done the right thing? What will happen when I see Carl again at Stuart's wedding?

Sally's voice breaks into my thoughts.

"There they are! Andy! Craig!"

The two lads trudge towards us, chatting away.

"Looks like they've made it up!" I laugh.

Sally sits down again.

"They're chalk and cheese, always have been — nothing in common at all." She shrugs. "But they're very fond of each other."

I gaze at the boys. Craig grabs his bucket and charges back into the sea. Andy retrieves his Harry Potter and lies down on his tummy.

"Nothing in common, but very fond of each other . . ."

Sally could be talking about Carl and me. Except that we were more than just fond of each other. I knew our feelings went deeper than that. I close my eyes, basking in the warmth of the sun.

Ten minutes later, I stand up slowly.

"I have to find a newsagent before they close," I say. "It was lovely meeting you!"

"And you!" Sally smiles. "Bye!"

LATER, back in my flat, I fill in the wedding reply card. *Lois regrets she will be unable to attend . . .*

Stuart will understand my absence — and so, one day, will Carl. He'll realise that the split was for the best. Suddenly, I am positive of that — I know I have done the right thing.

The constant bickering and compromising would have worn us both down in the end. I think of those little children, Craig and Andy — opposites, like Carl and me. Nothing in common. Except that when they grow up, they'll be free to go their separate ways. But getting married means being together for life . . .

My phone is ringing.

"Lois, it's Dawn, from work! A crowd of us are going for a meal tonight. How do you fancy joining us?" ■

Pretty In Pink

by
**Georgie
Foord.**

THE sound of the church bells brought the small grey-haired woman to the window. Bells on a Saturday meant that there was a wedding at the church up the road, and with a bit of luck she would see the bridal cars go by.

An immense ginger cat lay stretched full length in the sun on the window-sill. She ran her hand down his back, and his muscular tail, striped like a bell rope, flicked a small vase of lily of the valley behind him, sending it crashing to the floor.

"Hector! What am I going to do with you?" she scolded.

The heady scent of the flowers reached her, and she was transported back to the golden afternoon more than fifty years ago, when her dearest wish had been granted . . .

Lynne had a secret dream that she kept carefully hidden away. She

*Illustration by
Maggie Palmer.*

was sure that people would laugh if they knew.

Lynne longed with all her heart to be a bridesmaid. Unlike other girls in her class at school, she had no brothers or sisters or even cousins who might one day ask her to be a bridesmaid at their wedding, and when she looked in the mirror she knew she had no hope at all.

The problem was Lynne had to wear horrible thick glasses, with pink plastic frames, which were considered suitable for eight-year-old girls. She was a sensible child and knew that she needed her glasses, but how she hated them! Mum would try to cheer her up by saying she could have some pretty, grown-up frames when she was older, but Lynne wanted them now!

Most of the children in her class had got used to it, except for beastly Alfie Bates, who would sneakily try to trip her up, and hissed "Specky Four-Eyes!" behind her back when Miss Thompson wasn't listening.

Lynne pretended not to care, but she actually did mind rather a lot.

Nobody bothered to tell Lynne that her hair was the colour of shiny new conkers, which complemented a perfect creamy complexion with the merest dusting of golden freckles on her small snub nose.

Lynne had a scrapbook filled with wedding pictures cut from Mum's magazines. She studied the bridesmaids' frocks and tried to imagine herself dressed up like a princess. The brides' dresses, she thought, were pretty enough, but they were always white or cream, whilst the attendants could wear lots of different colours.

Lynne had no doubt which she liked best. Pink was her favourite: the colour of strawberry ice-cream, cherry blossom, and the geraniums in Grandma's front porch.

Whenever there was a wedding at the church in the village, Lynne would sit on the stone wall, longing to be a part of it all. She imagined what it would feel like to follow the bride up the aisle, to line up for all those photographs, and afterwards to ride in the big limousine.

She shared her dream with Tobias, their elderly Labrador, but no-one else knew of her heart's desire. Or so she thought.

MISS THOMPSON was Lynne's class teacher. She was quite old, at least thirty, Lynne thought, but more like a mum than a teacher. She wore mumsy clothes — tweed skirts and jumpers and flat shoes — but she was kind to Lynne. She gave her jobs to do like making sure there was enough chalk for the blackboard and seeing that the duster never got lost.

This made Lynne feel important, and she knew that Miss Thompson relied on her. Best of all, Miss Thompson wore big specs, too.

Then one day something exciting happened. When Miss Thompson had finished taking the morning register, she had some Very Important News.

"I want to tell you, children, that I am going to be married."

Everyone gasped. Miss Thompson went a bit pink.

"I am getting married to Mr Green, who teaches the Seniors."

There was silence. Beastly Alfie Bates sniggered, and Miss Thompson glared at him. Mr Green! But he was ancient, Lynne thought, and rather cross looking, and he had a bald patch on the top of his head.

"I am hoping that one of you girls might be able to help me out," Miss Thompson went on. "You see, I don't know anybody I could ask to be my bridesmaid."

LYNNE sat very still. But of course, there was no chance . . .

"Anybody who would like to be my bridesmaid, put up your hands!" Miss Thompson said. Eleven arms shot up.

"Me, Miss, please, Miss, I'll do it. Miss, choose me!"

Lynne sat on her hands, stared at her desk and screwed up her eyes, trying not to cry. Miss Thompson was sure to want somebody like Angela, with her blonde curls and big blue eyes.

Miss Thompson looked around the room.

"Lots of willing helpers, I see! But what about you, Lynne — wouldn't you like to be my bridesmaid?"

Near to tears, Lynne could only stare dumbly back. Miss Thompson looked thoughtful.

"Hmm!" she said. "I think I had better put all your names in a hat and draw one out — that would be the fairest way, don't you agree, girls?"

Miss Thompson spent the next few minutes scribbling names on little bits of paper. Then, in the absence of a suitable hat, she put them all in an empty biscuit tin which lived on the top shelf of the art cupboard. She popped out of the room to borrow Mrs Evans, the Head's secretary, to do the draw for them.

Miss Thompson shuffled the papers around, then held the tin out at arm's length. Mrs Evans put in her hand and drew one of the slips of paper out. She handed it to Miss Thompson.

"Oh, dear!" Miss Thompson said. "This says 'Lynne Jones'. I'm sorry, Lynne, your name seems to have got in by mistake. But don't you think you might be able to help me out, and be my bridesmaid on my big day?"

Lynne was almost speechless.

"Yes, Miss Thompson, thank you Miss Thompson," she managed to stutter.

"Oh, lucky you, Lynne!" Angela shouted.

With a little smile, Miss Thompson tipped the other pieces of paper into her bag and snapped it tight shut.

The great day arrived at last. The sun was shining in a pale blue-washed sky, with small puffball clouds chasing each other across the treetops. The churchyard was a mass of daffodils nodding approval, and Lynne stood at the church door, waiting for the bride.

Shivering with excitement, she looked down at her dress. It was the sweetest, palest pink, scattered with tiny silk rosebuds and real seed pearls. Round her neck hung the little silver locket Miss Thompson had given her as a memento of the day.

Mum had curled her hair around a circlet of pink and white rosebuds, and she carried a small posy of pink roses and lily-of-the-valley. Lynne buried her nose in the flowers and thought she had never smelled anything quite so heavenly.

A big shiny car with pink ribbons on the front pulled up at the church gate. Miss Thompson got out with a man whom Lynne knew must be Miss Thompson's dad.

Lynne hardly recognised her teacher. Her hair was swept up on top of her head and crowned with flowers, and she wore a beautiful creamy lace gown with a long filmy veil. Her bouquet was a grown-up version of Lynne's little posy.

"Oh, Miss Thompson, you look so beautiful!" she gasped.

"And you, Lynne, are quite the prettiest bridesmaid I could have imagined." Miss Thompson smiled.

The organ struck up the first notes of "Here Comes The Bride" and Lynne followed her teacher into the church and up the aisle, to where Mr Green was waiting. Even he looked different, Lynne thought, so happy and proud and really quite handsome after all, in his best suit. All the smiling people in the pews turned to watch them.

Everyone agreed it was absolutely the perfect wedding. The little bridesmaid looked after the bride's flowers so carefully, and helped her with her veil, and sang all the hymns at the top of her voice.

Listening to the words of the service, Lynne was fascinated to learn that Miss Thompson's first name was Muriel, and Mr Green was Ralph, which she thought rather dashing.

The bells were pealing their joyful message as they came out of the church. Angela and the others were waiting to throw confetti. Even Alfie Bates was there, and he let out a huge wolf-whistle which made Miss Thompson laugh. As she lined up in the sunshine to have her photograph taken, Lynne thought she was the luckiest and happiest girl in the world.

*   *   *   *

Lynne turned away from the window as the door opened behind her. A small sandy-haired girl erupted into the room.

"Hi, Granny! Guess what? I've just seen a wedding at the church and they came in a horse and cart! It was so cool!"

Her grandmother laughed.

"I know, Sophie, darling. They came past my window. I love weddings, too, you know! Did I ever tell you about the time I was a bridesmaid? I must have been just about your age, I suppose."

The little girl rolled her eyes to the heavens.

"Oh, Granny! You must have told me that story nearly a zillion trillion times! But I don't mind hearing it again."

Lynne picked up the grainy, black and white photograph from the sideboard and the little girl snuggled up to her on the sofa, pointing out the familiar faces as the story unfolded.

Hector, who never missed an opportunity to sit on a lap, jumped up to join them.

"That's you, Granny, and there's Miss Thompson and Mr Green. The lady in the funny hat is Mr Green's auntie and the fat man at the back is — um — Mr Thompson." She sighed with satisfaction.

"You were lucky, Granny. I wonder if I'll ever be a bridesmaid and have a fairy princess dress?"

"I shouldn't be a bit surprised if you did, lovey, a pretty girl like you. But it's time you were off home to your mum. Grandpa will be home from the allotment and wanting his tea."

The kitchen door opened and a tall, burly man came in, carrying a basket of vegetables.

"Mind my clean floor, Alfie!" Lynne warned. "Leave your boots on the mat. Hurry up and get washed, there's a cottage pie in the oven for you."

He grinned at her.

"Turned into a right bossy-boots, you have, Lynne Jones! But I loved you then and I always will."

He lifted her glasses from her nose and kissed her tenderly. ∎

The Important Things In Life

by Elizabeth Richards.

Illustration by Sally Rowe.

THE telephone call came shortly before teatime. Greg ignored the noise. He was watching the cricket on television, leaning forward on his elbows to follow the match as closely as possible. The sitting-room was dark, with the curtains drawn tightly to keep out the midsummer afternoon.

The telephone rang on and on, demanding to be answered, and eventually Greg's wife, Janet, swished through the french windows and rushed to the kitchen. A slice of yellow sunshine flashed across the television before the curtains settled back into long folds.

She threw Greg an exasperated glance as she passed. It was the same every year during the cricket season. He turned into a monosyllabic hermit with no time for anything except test scores and matches.

Greg frowned, focusing on the grey glow of the television once more. It was no good; he was distracted now. He rose from his chair with a grunt and padded through to the kitchen, where Janet was dropping the telephone receiver back into its cradle.

"That was Kate," she told him brightly.

Greg nodded and moved to look out of the window, wondering why his daughter had phoned. After all, she had visited only that morning.

"She's in a spot of bother, actually," Janet continued. "She's got her aromatherapy exam tomorrow and she was going to use Rosie, you know, her neighbour, as a model, but Rosie's not well and so she needs to find someone else . . ." She tailed off.

Greg turned to her, panicking suddenly.

"I hope you're not suggesting that I have to do it," he started indignantly.

"No, no! Kate wants me to stand in as the model. But there is one problem. She can't find a babysitter. I was going to look after Amy, but seeing as I'm now out of action she was hoping that maybe you would look after her."

For a second Greg was speechless.

"Me?" he finally squeaked. "What do I know about babies? Can't she take Amy with her?"

"Don't be ridiculous, Gregory!" Janet used his full name to show that she was annoyed. "Of course she can't, it's an exam! Anyway, it would be nice for you to get to know Amy. She's your only granddaughter, remember."

"How do you get to know a baby?" Greg muttered to himself. He leaned forward and stared across their rambling cottage garden.

"That yellow rose is dying, you know."

Janet gave a long sigh.

"You are such a grump." Then she was gone, back to the garden.

GREG couldn't sleep that night. The room was quiet and still, the air heavy around him. The only sound was Janet's slow breathing as she slept beside him. Rolling into her

Illustration by Kurt Ard.

91

back, Greg thought of her words earlier. Honestly, fancy suggesting that he should look after Amy. He knew nothing about babies! And there were two important matches on tomorrow!

His mind wandered back to his own childhood. His mother had been the person to look after him, teaching him to walk and read and write. His father would pop into the nursery after work to check he'd been good.

Then, of course, he grew up and went on to have his own children. Janet had been so good at looking after their babies, he remembered, and he was working such long hours when they were little.

He thought back to how he would arrive home just in time to read them a bedtime story. He'd never really needed to take care of them.

The next day dawned bright and sunny. Shortly after lunch, Greg was holed up indoors watching the cricket when the sharp jangle of keys sounded at the front door.

Kate stepped gingerly into the room and peered through the dim light. She was wearing a smart white dress and her long brown hair was pulled back neatly.

"Hello, Dad," she said, bending to kiss her father's cheek. "Mum said you'd look after Amy while we go to my exam."

Greg took a deep breath.

"Yes, well, circumstances and all that," he mumbled. "What do I have to do?"

"Nothing at all. Amy's been fed but I'll leave some milk in the kitchen just in case. She's asleep now so she'll probably be that way until we get back." Kate pushed the pram into the sitting-room and parked it beside her father. "Thanks, Dad, you're great."

Janet came bustling in from the garden. She tugged on her sunhat and turned to her husband.

"Well, we're off now. See you later." She disappeared before Greg could reply. He looked at his daughter.

"We'll be back in two hours," she promised him, before following her mother. Greg heard the quiet click of the front door as it closed behind them.

SO, he was in charge now. He peered into the pram to look at his sleeping granddaughter and then turned his attention back to the cricket.

Ten minutes later, Greg was distracted by a strange noise. He looked around him and, seeing nothing, poked his nose over the edge of the pram.

Amy's little round face stared back at him, eyes wide and questioning. Then she screwed up her face and started to cry.

"Drat," Greg muttered, "so much for staying asleep." He poked his finger at the baby and tried to tickle her under the chin, but she cried louder.

Remembering something he'd seen Janet do years before, Greg stood and, taking hold of the pram, began to rock it backwards and forwards.

"No, that's not going to work, is it?" he said. "How about some milk? Are you hungry?"

He fetched the bottle from the kitchen and pushed it towards Amy's face. She twisted her head from it, fat tears bursting from her eyes. Greg set the bottle down on the table and, rummaging madly through the bag beneath the pram, yanked out a teddy bear. He waved it in front of Amy, who screamed. Her damp face was crinkled and red from crying.

"What do you want?" Greg finally demanded in despair. He rubbed his eyes and peered again at the child. Then he bent forward and carefully lifted her out of the pram.

"Hush, hush, Amy," he pleaded. The child's cries quietened as he cradled her awkwardly in his arms. Taking a furtive glance about him, Greg sang her name softly under his breath.

"Amy, Amy, Amy," he crooned. "Don't cry!"

Amy gulped and stared at him. He shifted her in his arms and, holding her tightly, wiped away her tears with his sweater. The baby gurgled and rubbed her face against the woollen sleeve.

"There, that's better," Greg said, pleased at having the situation under control again. He settled Amy back in the pram and slumped into his armchair once more. He pushed his knuckles into his eyes for a second before focusing his attention on the television screen. He'd lost track of the match now.

Within a minute, another cry from the pram pierced his concentration. It was no good, he thought. He'd never be able to follow the game. Rising from his chair, he snapped off the television and the room was plunged momentarily into quiet darkness.

He lifted Amy up and paced the room with her, trying to distract her from crying. He crossed to the window and pulled the curtains open. Sunlight rushed in, making them both blink.

"Look here," Greg said, noticing a framed photograph on the window-sill. "Here's your mum when she was just a bit older than you."

He stared at the fading image as though seeing it for the first time.

"You look just like her, you know," he added quietly.

He wiped dust from the frame and set the picture back in its place. Amy leaned towards the sunlight and grabbed at a flower through the glass.

"Want to take a look outside?" Greg asked her. Shooting a regretful look at the blank television screen, he stepped through the french windows and out on to the grass.

Fountains Abbey, near Ripon

The sun's warmth fell on his face and he instinctively turned towards it, closing his eyes against the brightness. It's been too long since I was out here, he thought, surprising himself. Amy gurgled and wriggled in his arms and he shifted his attention back to her.

"Look at the hens, Amy!" He pointed up the garden and her bright eyes followed his finger. The fat orange hens were pecking through the dusty flower-beds, scratching and clucking happily. Amy giggled and waved her hands at them, and they scattered crossly.

"And look here, this swing used to belong to your mum," Greg continued.

The wooden swing hung from a branch of the great oak tree. He pushed it and the creaking ropes puffed out clouds of dust.

"I remember when your mum used this swing. She was on it all the time, couldn't get her away from it. One day you'll play on it, when you're a bit bigger."

Greg gave a low chuckle when he realised what he had said.

"You're turning me into a right old softy," he growled at the baby.

They walked long slow laps of the garden, looking at the tiniest flowers and the big old trees. Greg showed Amy where the swallows nested each summer and where the butterflies liked to drink nectar from the buddleia. The hens followed them, chattering gently amongst themselves.

SET in a sheltered valley three miles from Ripon, the World Heritage site of Fountains Abbey is one of Europe's most historic places.

The Cistercian abbey, closed by Henry VIII, still glories in ornamental lakes, a mediaeval deer park and a Jacobean hall.

This superb setting, so steeped in history, makes for a fascinating and informative day out.

J. CAMPBELL KERR.

"Better get you indoors," he said finally. "This sun is too bright for babies, it'll burn your skin."

THE sitting-room was cool and dark. Greg sat in his armchair and tucked Amy beside him. She curled up her hands and feet and snuggled against his arm.

Greg closed his eyes. He felt sleepy suddenly. His eyes were tired from the bright sunshine and his arms ached from Amy's weight. The baby smelled sweet and powdery beside him, her little chest rising and falling with sleeping breaths.

Greg's mind floated back to Kate's childhood, so many years ago. Was this what he'd been missing out on all that time he'd been working in the bank? All those hours spent in that dusty office, working on figures and accounts, when he could have been at home with the children.

A sudden noise woke him from his snooze. He looked up, startled, to find Kate and Janet peering round the door at him. Then he looked down at Amy, who was fast asleep in his arms. He brushed a grass seed from her hair.

Kate took the sleeping baby from him and carefully laid her back in the pram. Then she bent and kissed her father.

"Thanks, Dad," she said. "You've done a great job."

Greg squeezed her arm.

"Any time," he told her. "I enjoyed having her here."

Kate left quietly and Greg sat for a moment in the dark before getting up from his chair. He could hear Janet busying herself in the kitchen and went through to find her.

Janet smiled as he entered the kitchen. She was making a pot of tea. Greg could see the steam curling up from the pot. He set out cups and saucers before speaking.

"How did Kate's exam go?"

"It went really well. She passed with flying colours and the tutor said she was a natural." She poured the tea and passed Greg's cup to him. "Why aren't you watching the cricket?"

Greg sipped the hot tea.

"It's too nice to watch television," he admitted eventually. He moved to stand beside her at the window and they stared out at the garden together. Beams of early evening sunshine lay across the grass in long stripes. Janet slipped her hand into Greg's and squeezed his fingers tightly.

"You're not such an old grump after all," she said softly, looking up at her husband.

Greg pulled her closer and put his arm around her.

"You know what, Janet? I do believe I was mistaken. Your yellow rose — it's not dying at all. I think all it needs is a bit of love." ■

Illustration by
Pat Gregory.

Perfect Partners

by Ginny
Swart.

SARAH stared gloomily at the room full of elderly folk enjoying the tea break between bingo sessions at the seniors' club, and wished she could be somewhere else. The small amount of money she earned by assisting with the teas every Thursday afternoon didn't make up for the fact that she was missing a good session with her best mates over at Marilyn's house.

Marilyn's mum sold cosmetics and gave her daughter loads of samples to try out, so afternoons at Marilyn's were always a giggle.

"More tea, Mr Macmillan?"

"Thank you, Sarah, my dear, I believe I will have just a half."

He was a sweetie, full of fun and charming in an old-fashioned way, standing up when her grandmother came to the tea table and holding out her chair as she sat down.

Older men did stuff like that, she'd noticed, but if any boy did that for her,

97

she'd die of embarrassment.

Not that she would ever meet any boys if she carried on working at the seniors' club. Lucky Marilyn, who helped on Saturdays at her aunt's café, boasted that she met hundreds of boys, really cool ones.

She claimed that half the members of the school football team had come in and chatted her up while she served them cappuccinos, including Rory the captain whom everybody fancied — but Sarah didn't believe her. Marilyn always exaggerated.

"Any musical contributions for our dinner-dance next month?"

Mrs Thomas was in charge of the ancient record player in the corner and was going from table to table with a list.

"We have a Frank Sinatra on loan from Annie Howell, and Mr Phillips has promised us a Perry Como, although he says it's a bit scratched. I'm looking for some nice dance music with a big band, if you know what I mean."

"Like Denny Dennis with Roy Fox?" Her grandmother spoke up unexpectedly.

"Oh, yes, wasn't he a lovely singer?" Mrs Thomas agreed. "He was such a heart-throb, too. Those eyes! Does anyone have any of his records?"

No-one had. Sarah wasn't surprised; she'd never even heard of Denny Dennis.

Tea over, the club members took their seats at the bingo tables and Sarah hurried through the washing up. She might still have time for half an hour with the gang.

✳   ✳   ✳   ✳

The following weekend Sarah was helping her grandmother tidy the boxes on top of the cupboard in her bedroom.

"Who's this fancy fellow, Gran? Grandad when he was young?"

Sarah was going through a box of old papers and birthday cards, and held up a studio portrait of a good-looking man with a long thin face and dark hair slicked back from his high forehead.

"Goodness me, no." Mrs Stewart was delighted with her find. "That's Denny Dennis! Wherever did you find it?"

"Here, in this packet of photos."

"Denny was born here in Derby, you know, and he was really famous. During the war, and afterwards . . ."

She smoothed the photo, grown slightly brown over the years, and her voice trailed off, remembering.

"You must have been a proper fan — you've even got his autograph!" There was a confident scribble in the bottom corner.

To Rose Agnew from Denny Dennis.

"I was one of his biggest admirers when I was a girl. I went to a concert once, when he was singing with Roy Fox and his band. Me and your great-aunt Margaret, we queued for hours for those tickets. He was the most wonderful singer."

Sarah couldn't picture her grandmother standing screaming inside the concert hall, almost crying with excitement, like she and Marilyn had done when Westlife came to town.

"We had very good seats, right near the front. Margaret said he winked at her, but I was never sure."

Seats at a pop concert? Weird.

"He was such a gentleman. He wore the loveliest suits, so well-cut, and of course when the war came, he joined up and then he sang in uniform, for the troops — him and Vera Lynn."

"I've heard of her, I think," Sarah said uncertainly.

"We were heartbroken when he sailed off to America and joined another big band . . . who was it now . . . oh, yes, Tommy Dorsey. But he made lovely records there, too. I used to have them all. 'These Foolish Things' . . . 'Stardust' . . . Oh, he had such a beautiful voice. We used to dance to his songs when we were newly wed, your grandad and me."

All Sarah remembered about her grandfather was a bent old man with a loud hacking cough. It came from being down the mines all those years, her mother had said. She'd been only seven when her grandmother came to live with them and she couldn't imagine life without her.

"So what happened to your records, Gran?"

"Oh, you know. They broke, or got scratched. After your grandad died and I sold our home, I gave them all to the jumble sale."

"Gran! How could you bear to do that?" Sarah would never, ever part with her Justin Timberlake CD.

Mrs Stewart smiled wistfully.

"All that music was part of my life, but so long ago. Besides, there's no space in my room here for our great big old record player. It was built into a stand all of its own, made of oak, with a lid that lifted up and two shelves underneath to store the records. We had quite a big collection."

"Just Denny Dennis?"

"No, we had Frank Sinatra, too . . . but I didn't like him as much. Your grandad always preferred cowboy songs. I used to give him a Gene Autry or a Tex Ritter record for his birthday every year. I think he fancied himself on a horse wearing one of those big white hats." She started to sing softly.

"There's a yellow Rose of Texas, I'm going for to see . . ."

Then she laughed.

"Your grandad always sang that song to me."

"Show me the other photos, Gran. Who's this, then?"

They settled on the bed, her grandmother sifting through the photos and naming them, sometimes with difficulty. Auntie Pam, Uncle Fred, Grandfather Agnew with Milly. They were people Sarah had never heard of, many of them no longer alive.

Somehow, gazing at their stiff, serious faces and their old-fashioned clothes gave her a pleasant sensation of roots. Somewhere, in Canada and Australia and even down in London, she had a big extended family of second cousins and great-aunts by marriage. One day she'd travel the world and look them up.

Meanwhile, she knew exactly what she'd give her grandmother for her birthday next week.

FINDING a recording of Denny Dennis proved impossible. No-one at the music shop had ever heard of him. Tommy Dorsey, yes, under the Vintage Big Band Selection of CDs, but no Denny Dennis.

"Try the internet, love," the assistant advised. "They've got a lot of old stuff. Collectibles."

"You mean records?"

"You're not going to find that singer on anything but Bakelite," he said. "Old seventy-eights, they'll be."

Of course, the seniors' club has that record player, she remembered. So it would be better than trying to find a CD anyway.

Not holding out much hope of success, Sarah went home and typed the singer's name into a search engine on her computer. To her amazement, Denny Dennis was mentioned often. Several sites offered second-hand records for sale — tunes with odd names like "It's A Lovely Day Tomorrow", and "You'd Be So Nice To Come Home To".

A few records were described as *Fair condition, slight crinkling at the edge of disc,* or *Well-loved collector's item, original sleeve,* which didn't sound too encouraging.

In the end, she chose two which claimed *Excellent condition.* One had "Hear My Song, Violetta" on one side and "Serenade Of Napoli" on the other, and the second, "Did You Ever See A Dream Walking" and "Smoke Gets In Your Eyes". She hoped her grandmother would appreciate the thought even if she couldn't play them at home.

✳   ✳   ✳   ✳

"Who'd have thought Gran would be so thrilled!" Sarah said happily. "And wasn't it lucky that the seniors' club has a record player that plays them? I didn't realise that different-sized records played different speeds."

Love-In-Bloom

Will we remember, as the years go by,
How you and I strolled in the park today,
With Scamp? And how the limpid sky
Was softly blue, and a stillness lay
Over daisied grass, and silent trees,
With sunbeams caught in their green canopies?

Will we remember flower-beds, summer-bright,
All glorious hues; how the very air
Was Sabbath calm? I think we might —
And how those butterflies were everywhere?
Then, we heard the music; how it seemed
To set the seal on all we dreamed . . .

Your hand in mine, I felt such bliss,
As, to the trumpet's call, we moved along,
I'd never known I could feel like this,
And only hope that, like an old, sweet song,
The memory lingers, and will ever stay
Deep in our hearts, no matter what betide,
For this has been the loveliest day,
The day you asked me, "Will you be my bride?"
— Kathleen O'Farrell.

"It was very thoughtful of you to find just the right present, darling," her mother said. Her own gift of a new hot-water bottle and some chocolates hadn't been greeted with anything like such a gasp of sheer pleasure. "And now you've got a job as a DJ for the big night. Who'd have thought that?"

Sarah grinned at her mother's teasing, but winced inwardly. Although she loved her grandmother and really didn't mind helping, she just hoped none of her friends would ever find out. It would be just too embarrassing!

The club members had started practising a few steps after bingo every week in preparation for the annual dance. Sarah had been roped in to change the records, announce the next tune and put the records away in the fragile brown-paper covers and had promised to do it for the dance, too.

"All the cola and crisps you can manage, young lady, and maybe you could find a handsome partner, should you wish to trip the — er — light fantastic." Mr Macmillan's eyes twinkled at her.

"Go on, Mr Macmillan, you won't catch me doing the foxtrot!" Sarah giggled, but thought privately that Mr Macmillan should stick to dancing with people his own age, like Gran.

Gran looked so graceful, dancing with him. All those quick little steps and twirling about didn't look too bad, actually. For older people, of course.

"There are some very good dancers at the club." Her grandmother smiled. "Although, of course, none of them are as good as your grandfather was. You should try it yourself one day."

"I don't think so, Gran!" Sarah grimaced. "Thanks all the same."

"Every girl should know a bit of ballroom dancing," her grandmother said calmly. "You never know when you might be called upon to waltz. Or foxtrot. This would be a good place to learn."

"Honestly, Gran, nobody my age dances like that any more."

"You'd be surprised." Mrs Stewart smiled serenely. "Arthur — Mr Macmillan, I mean — tells me his grandson has been taking lessons."

That grandson must be a real wimp, Sarah thought.

ON the evening of the dance, she was about to leave the house with her grandmother, who was resplendent in a long blue velvet skirt and silky black top, when she was stopped at the door.

"Surely you're not coming dressed in jeans? This is a special occasion, you know, dear. Why not wear that pretty red outfit you wore to Sally's wedding?"

She'd never liked that dress, but she went upstairs rather unwillingly and did as her grandmother suggested, adding a touch of lipstick before returning and doing a little pirouette for approval.

"Better, Gran?"

"Much better. Very suitable."

Sarah sighed and followed her into the taxi.

THE Seniors' Club had been transformed with streamers of crêpe paper and balloons, the tables laid with red cloths and sparkling with glasses. Mrs Stewart found her name-tag on a table and sat down, and Sarah went to the record player in the corner to start some background music while people arrived. Everyone was dressed up, the men in dinner jackets, some with cummerbunds, and looked quite different.

On the stroke of eight, Mrs Phillips waved to her urgently and she put on the first record, turning the volume up so it could be heard above the pleasant hubbub of conversation. Perry Como was singing "Magic Moments".

His voice sounds like honey, she thought suddenly, so smooth. And you could hear every word he sang, as though he'd had speech lessons.

People immediately smiled at each other and rose from the tables to take their partners. She noticed her grandmother stayed seated, watching the door. Ah, there was Mr Macmillan at last, in a bow tie and shiny lapels, coming in and sitting down at Gran's table. But who was that boy standing next to him?

Sarah suddenly recognised him and went bright red. She'd never imagined that the school football captain was Mr Macmillan's grandson! Tall, good-looking and at least eighteen years old, Rory Macmillan also played lead guitar in a band called Dead Penguins. Rory was extremely cool, about as cool as you could get without freezing solid.

And here she was working in the seniors' club dressed as though she was off to Sunday school. Sarah swallowed hard and bent over the record player, hoping he hadn't seen her.

But he walked over and watched her place the needle on the track of Denny Dennis singing "Stardust", her hand trembling slightly. And then he spoke.

"May I have the pleasure of this dance?"

Sarah nearly fainted and her first impulse was to refuse.

"Well, all right," she mumbled awkwardly, and joined him on the dance floor. She tried not to notice that her grandmother and Mr Macmillan, now making a handsome couple, were smiling happily in their direction.

I'm in the arms of Rory Macmillan! Exulted, Sarah tried to keep her toes out from under his feet. This must be the handsome partner Mr Macmillan was talking about. Wow, just wait till I tell the others tomorrow. Rory Macmillan does ballroom dancing!

Suddenly, ballroom dancing made a whole lot of sense, although it certainly wasn't as easy as her gran made it look.

Rory danced like a dream — she simply had to have lessons. Maybe Mr Macmillan would teach her! ■

where I belong

by Penelope Alexander.

DON'T be too long, Mari, *bach*," Mam called. "Dan will be here soon."

"All right, Mam!"

Thoughtfully, Mari Duggan closed the door and headed off along the beach. Almost at once, she found a large spiral shell stranded above the tideline, and cradling it in her hand, she climbed high into the dunes.

As was usual in the week of Dan's visit, all the talk had been of him. Mari's family loved to see him. But this time the tale might change, as everyone well knew.

Mari wasn't thinking of stories as she held the sea shell and gazed out to sea, but of real life.

Our Man Dan, as the family affectionately called him, had lodged with the Duggans when he'd first arrived from Australia, and had been a frequent visitor ever since.

He was also the young man who'd managed to turn Mari's life upside down with a single question.

"Will you marry me?"

Mari sat down among the dune grasses, endlessly tracing the patterns on the spiralled shell with one finger. The surface was dusty and dull, but she knew how it would alter if she put it in the sea, where it belonged.

Dan's response to his own question had been simple. They loved each other, and they should be together.

"What's so complicated?" he'd asked.

"Nothing — if only the world was smaller," Mari had replied, snuggled against Dan's shoulder. "Mam thinks you're lovely, and even Dad agrees I should go with you. But honestly, Dan, the thought of leaving everything I've ever known and moving to the other side of the world — it scares me."

"Travel's part of life these days, Mari. How else would I have met the most beautiful girl in the world?"

"I never thought of going so far away, Dan."

"You know I'd take care of you . . ."

Dan hugged her close with his free arm, and Mari patted his hand.

"I know, Dan. It's not you, it's me. Where would I belong?"

"You'd be the girl who belonged with me from the first moment I saw her," Dan murmured, bestowing a gentle kiss on her cheek.

Instead of feeling reassured, Mari felt an odd panic folding over her. It was like listening to the booming echoes of the sea inside a large shell, and not knowing where the sounds came from.

Finally she forced herself to speak.

"I love you, too, Dan."

SHE knew that much was true. But could she depend on those feelings? They were certainly strong enough to sweep her into Dan's arms. But were they also sincere enough to sustain a marriage on the other side of the world, where she knew no-one and was miles away from all her family and friends?

"You'll have to trust yourself," Dan said, as if he had read her thoughts, "as well as me."

Mari stood up, brushing down her skirt, knowing Dan had stated her problem as neatly as if it had been packed into a mermaid's purse.

"We'll see," she said, covering the wobble in her voice. "How long will you be staying this time?"

"Another three months or so, until the engineering work I'm doing here ends."

"Twelve weeks?" Mari whispered, her mouth drying.

Dan stood and took her in his arms.

"Stop panicking! Nothing is written in stone except 'I love you'. It's ridiculous to imagine we'll stop loving each other. It's just that, this time, I don't want us to say 'Goodbye until the next visit' when I have to leave."

They had walked silently, hand in hand, the beautiful shells rolling in the water at their feet. Mari wondered whether Australian sea shells could be so very different.

Dan pulled her towards him, his eyes serious.

"Promise you'll let me know, either way, when I come again?"

IT seemed she'd been sitting in the dunes for ages, watching the waves topple on to the wide beach so far off that their sound barely seemed like a whisper.

The spiky shadows of the dune grasses lengthened. The tide came in, and the sand cooled. Dan would be here soon. Smoothing the spiral with her fingers one last time, Mari felt there was only one answer she could give him.

She heard a shout and Dan came into view, his feet toiling in the soft sand.

"Hi," he said, breathless, reaching her side with a final heroic effort. "Your mam says to bring you in for tea. Welshcakes — your favourite. It smells like heaven in the kitchen . . ."

He was talking quickly, as if he feared an awkward gap might appear without warning in their conversation. Mari began to speak, but Dan put his finger on her lips.

"Don't," he said, his voice tender. "Let's walk to the sea first, like we always do. It's so good to see you."

As they had done countless times, they linked hands to scramble across the dunes.

"What's that?" Dan asked, looking at Mari's hand.

"Just some old shell."

He helped her over the last clump of dune grass and down on to the beach.

"Race you!" Mari called, hopping as she kicked off her shoes.

She ran fast, turning to face him once she reached the waves, kicking the spray high and laughing. Dan dodged her splashes, his feet leaving smooth, broad prints in the wet sand. He caught Mari by the waist and they spun among the shallow ripples like a whirligig.

Mari felt the shell tumble from her hand.

When the world stopped revolving, she looked, breathless, to see where the shell had fallen. It took a long time to spot it.

The shell dripped on Dan's shirt as she handed it to him. It was no longer dull. The sea had painted it every shade from yellow to deepest orange-red, and its surface was glossy with reflections.

"Shells are best where they belong," Dan said, replacing it carefully. He gathered both Mari's hands close and held them against his damp shirt, forcing her to look up.

Mari saw that the dearest eyes in the world were waiting, calmly, and would understand whatever she wanted to say.

"That's what I thought, too," she said. "The sea shell helped me decide where I belong, Dan, and I know that will always be with you." ■

W HAT'S wrong with the lass?"
Peggy was sitting reading in her chair by the fire, when her
great-granddaughter, Laura, burst in with that look on her face
which boded trouble.

Hattie rolled her eyes and shook her head.

"We'll find out soon enough, Mother, I expect."

She looked towards Laura, already at the table and helping herself to the
scones Hattie had just taken out of the oven.

It was obvious something was wrong, which surprised neither of the two

Follow Your Dreams

by Susie Riggott.

Illustration by Majken Thorsen.

older ladies. Sparks often flew when Laura was around!

"I'll put the kettle on." Hattie sighed. It looked like they were in for a long session. When did Laura ever arrive at tea-time, other than to dispose of Hattie's home-made cakes and pour out her troubles?

Peggy laid down the magnifying glass she'd been using. Her eyes were watering again — what a nuisance! She wiped them with the hanky she carried in her apron pocket for that purpose. Peggy still liked to wear her apron — it gave her the appearance of industry, at least.

"Aren't you going to tell us?" she asked Laura, a little waspishly.

"It's nothing." Laura had finished one scone and was already reaching for another. "Nothing. Only . . . it's not fair!"

"I didn't think it would be fair," Hattie interjected. It never was. Laura's life was full of unfairness, which she protested against long and volubly.

"They needn't think I'm staying on at school, because I'm not!"

"Aren't you, love?"

"No, and no-one can make me!"

"I'm sure no-one would even begin to try . . ."

"What does the girl say?" Peggy shouted. She was inclined to deafness and, like many who are hard of hearing, appeared to think everyone else was, too. Her hearing aid whined and hummed.

Deftly, Hattie leaned across and made some minor adjustments.

"Better, Mother?"

"Give over fiddling, woman — I can't make out what's wrong with the girl."

"I said I'm leaving school, Great-grandma!"

"Are you sure, darling?" Hattie interjected quickly, seeing the look on Peggy's face as the news sank in. "Isn't it rather a big step?"

If she sounded surprised herself, she was, since Laura was such a bright girl.

"I'm fed up with school . . ." Laura began.

"We all get a little fed-up sometimes."

Hattie hardly dared to look at Peggy.

"No! I mean really, *really* fed-up." Laura put all the passion only a sixteen-year-old could put into her voice. "I want to earn some money."

"Have you talked this over with your mum?"

"She won't listen."

"Perhaps she's thinking of your long-term future, darling?"

Laura frowned. She didn't need Hattie to point out that her mother might have a point. She'd come for some tea and sympathy, not more of the same she'd received at home! She looked across at Great-grandmother Peggy, who'd been remarkably quiet, given the subject in question.

"Young lady . . ." Peggy began, seeing the look. "Young lady, I've something to say to you!"

"Drink your tea, Mother," Hattie said, sensing trouble.

"But . . ."

"Later, dear."

Peggy subsided. The tea was only lukewarm. Didn't Hattie know to warm the pot? She was a good girl, though, on the whole.

Now, what were they talking about? Education? Education! How could Laura talk of turning her back on education? Wasn't it for life?

Abruptly, Laura, Hattie, this neat little terraced house, the front room where they were sitting, no longer existed for Peggy. She was young again, younger even than Laura.

How clearly she remembered the day in question — strange, considering she could hardly remember what was said from one minute to another.

Emotions tumbled through her mind. It was the day she'd left home, the day she left school firmly behind her. How keenly she'd felt it — the excitement, the grown-upness of it . . . even, she admitted it, the terror.

She'd been fourteen.

THE carrier set her down at the bottom of the road, called a cheery goodbye and urged his horses on. Peggy picked up her case and began to walk up the hill, trying to ignore the fact her stomach was tied in knots and her hands were damp with fear.

You're practically grown-up, Peggy Milligan, she told herself sternly. It's time you left home.

Since Mam had had the twins, there were simply too many mouths to feed — she had to stand on her own two feet! And if Miss Baker, her teacher, said she could have stayed on at school, even gone on to one of those big fancy universities . . . well, it just wasn't to be!

How could Mam ever have afforded to finance Peggy through years of study? Peggy had to face the fact with as much resignation as she could muster, even though that went against her nature — she hadn't a resigned bone in her body. But there wasn't enough food to go round at home.

She'd brought her books with her, all the same, tied up in string and tucked in a corner of her suitcase. Surely even kitchen-maids got time to themselves?

Seizing her courage, she marched straight up the drive to the big imposing house at the top, and pulled on the bell.

It seemed to take an interminably long time to open. How she longed to run away! But what would Mam say if she bolted straight back home again, after all the trouble of getting her here?

She heard footsteps at last. Peggy's heart seemed to be beating fit to burst, and her grip on the case tightened.

The door swung open, and a young man's face appeared. It was a nice face, but younger than she'd been expecting.

Strangely, the youth took one look at the trim little figure on the doorstep, the sunlight shining on her bright red hair, and burst out laughing.

Peggy frowned, her cheeks growing pink.

"Good afternoon!" she said forcefully, in her best posh voice.

"You're the new girl, aren't you? We've been expecting you." He seemed to take some sort of delight in her annoyance. "You won't half cop it, coming round to the front!"

The smile on his face and the twinkle in his eyes belied his words. She could have taken offence, but didn't. On a second look, he really had a nice face, which she couldn't help smiling back at. He came outside, and pulled the door shut behind him.

"I'm Sam Kettle, and I do the boots. I saw you coming up the drive from upstairs — I wouldn't have dared open the front door otherwise. I'll show you the back way round to the kitchen, if you like."

He held out a hand, which Peggy shook solemnly.

It was one of those moments in her life she never forgot. Sam Kettle putting her right — how many times was he to do that in her life?

He was already disappearing round the side of the house. Peggy followed him and, for the umpteenth time that day, told herself firmly she wasn't nervous, which she was, of course. How she longed for the school-room and the comfort of familiarity . . .

IT was two weeks later, and Peggy had never been so tired in all her short life. She sat at the table in the servants' hall, her head in a book — literally so. It was the evening, and she'd an hour to herself. A whole blissful hour!

She had intended to get down to some work at last, only her eyelids felt so heavy. She'd only closed them momentarily. Where had all that time gone?

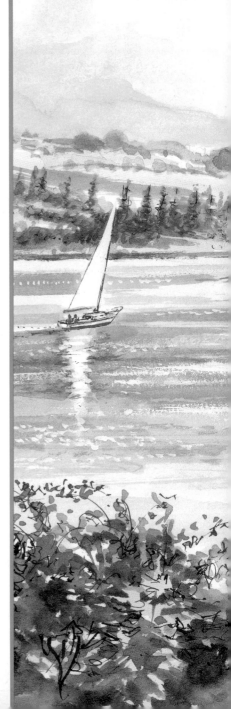

**Taf Fechan,
Brecon Beacons**

Peggy sat upright. It was nearly ten. Cook would be waiting for her hot chocolate, and there was still the servants' table to lay for breakfast in the morning.

Her hands, red raw, lay flat on the table in front of her. They didn't even look like her hands any more, except for the nails, bitten down to the quick. Mam would have skinned her alive if she'd seen the state they were in.

She had been rushed off her feet since she came here — scrubbing the stone kitchen floor until it gleamed, making up the fires in the mornings, peeling vegetables, scouring pots and pans.

All those pots! Peggy dreamed of them at nights, safe in her cramped little room at the very top of the house.

Cook said that if she kept up the good work, she'd let her help take the teas up in the morning.

Peggy smiled a little bitterly. What had happened to all her hopes and dreams?

The pinnacle of achievement, apparently, was taking tea to folk who were perfectly able to get up and make their own.

Better not let Cook hear her say that, though! It was . . . what was the word? Subversive! A good word, subversive. Miss Baker would be proud of her using that.

"Have you managed to get much done?" Sam breezed into the room, smiling as always.

Peggy had a soft spot for Sam

DEEP in the Brecon Beacons National Park lies the large upland forest of Taf Fechan. Planted around reservoirs, it's a great place to find secluded picnic spots and resting places.

The long-distance Taff Trail, from Brecon to Cardiff, passes through this area, with particularly beautiful views including panoramas of the mountains.

Why not lose yourself in this glorious wilderness?

J. CAMPBELL KERR.

already; he'd really helped her to settle in. She missed Mam so, as well as Tom and the twins and Eileen and little Betty. She also missed the cosy little school-room and her books.

"I've got nothing done, Sam Kettle," she said tartly, getting to her feet and yawning.

It didn't do to think of home too much. This was her home now, hard as that idea was to take in.

"I'll have to get it done on Wednesday," she said firmly. It was her afternoon off, and Peggy was desperately looking forward to it.

"Wednesday?" Sam frowned. "Oh, but . . ." He stopped and looked at her in some confusion.

"What's wrong with Wednesday?"

"There's a brass band in the park!" Sam spoke in a rush, his cheeks slightly red. "I thought we could go together. We've been stuck in all week. It might put a little colour back in your cheeks — you're beginning to look all pale and drawn. You should forget those silly old books — give yourself a bit of a break!"

She knew they weren't silly old books. They were important books, forming a gateway which opened on to an immense, spacious garden she'd only glimpsed far in the distance. It was beautiful, full of huge, green, leafy trees and brilliantly coloured flowers she couldn't even begin to guess the name of.

People like Peggy had to fight to get there, and it was hard going. It wasn't that she was turning her back on it, but somehow it just wasn't the same without Miss Baker urging her on, filling her head with tales of red-brick colleges and wonderful libraries and things to do with your life that seemed like a dream to Peggy.

But dreams didn't put food on the table, nor clothes on your back, though. They couldn't send much-needed money home to Mam, struggling to feed five children younger than Peggy, nor make Cook her hot chocolate even when you were dog-tired and longing for bed and had to be up at five in the morning to lay all the fires.

Peggy frowned, and looked long and hard at the book still open and waiting on the table. The breath seemed to rush out of her body as she slowly reached out one hand and closed it.

The sound echoed through the room, and in her head, the gate of her dream garden clanged shut, too.

"I promise I'll get back to you!" she told the book silently. "If it's the last thing I ever do in life! I'm not giving up on you!"

She turned to Sam and smiled gravely.

"I'll go with you, Sam, if you like."

114

To a real garden, full of real flowers. Well, she was here, in the real world. There were compensations . . .

I'VE always loved flowers," Peggy whispered.

"What's that, Mother?"

"Flowers . . . oh, take no notice!" Peggy cried, returning abruptly to the present.

"I was just telling Laura about your degree, Mother."

"Oh, that?" Despite the apparent dismissiveness of her tone, Peggy looked towards the photograph that had pride of place on the mantelpiece.

She'd never forgotten her promise, and she had never given up on her dream of a degree — nor had she ever guessed how long she would wait to fulfil it!

There she was in her cap and gown, a mere flibbertigibbet of seventy-five, wisps of grey hair escaping from under her mortar board.

Sam had always loved her hair; he'd loved every bit of her. Fifty happy years they'd shared! Even if he hadn't lived long enough to see her graduate, she knew how proud he would have been. Bless him!

And bless the Open University . . .

"Fancy you doing a degree, Great-grandma!"

Laura had heard this tale so many times, and never tired of it, for she'd been too young to remember the great event at the time. And now Great-grandma was even older — so ancient, Laura could hardly comprehend it.

She bounced up from the table, and moved across to the little bent figure in the chair. At once, she found her hands clasped between Peggy's own. She could feel the life still in them. So much life that it made you stop and think. What could it be like to be so old?

"All I'll say to you, young lady . . ." Peggy's old eyes gleamed ". . . is be grateful you have a choice."

There wasn't, after all, anything else to say. Everyone should have the chance to make up their own mind — it was called growing up. Didn't she know that better than anyone?

❋   ❋   ❋   ❋

Peggy and Hattie watched Laura go. It was as if a light had gone out of the room.

"I'd love her to go to university," Peggy whispered softly, almost to herself.

"I know you would, Mother," Hattie said. "But you're right. At least she has a choice."

Peggy subsided back into a chair, a frail little figure bursting with vitality.

She returned to her book, her mind still full of flowers . . . ■

Illustration by Len Thurston.

Blind Date

by Tanya A. Stead.

JENNA sat waiting in booth number nine, sipping at her soft drink, scolding herself for ever trusting her friends . . . again. It had been almost a year since she'd broken up with her long-time boyfriend, and recently her friends had been setting her up on blind dates, trying to get her back into the dating scene.

On this latest disastrous date, the unknown guy, Brad, was already thirty minutes late.

Jenna looked at her watch. Five more minutes, she thought, surveying the small café around her. Couples everywhere. She sighed.

She did want someone new. She simply hadn't found anyone yet. Her friends were only doing this out of concern for her, and at first she'd complied, knowing it made them happy to feel like they were helping.

But it was really getting beyond a joke. The potential dates had been getting progressively worse, and Mr Half An Hour Late was the final straw.

Jenna grabbed her bag and stood up. There was a phone at the back of the café — she could call her friends, tell them Brad hadn't shown up, and ask them to meet her now rather than tonight, as they'd planned.

She'd started dialling their number when she spotted a tall man with dark brown hair rush through the door and make his way quickly to booth nine. He slumped down in the chair, glanced around the room, and heaved a sigh.

Hanging up the phone, Jenna walked back over to the table.

"Brad?" she asked the man, trying her best not to sound too angry.

116

He looked up, relief flooding his face.

"Oh, I'm so glad you're still here. My car broke down and I couldn't get a cab and I caught two buses and ran the rest of the way and I know how late I am but . . ." His words tumbled together, leaving Jenna wondering if she should even give him a chance. "I'm so sorry."

He sounded sincere, and at least if she went through with this date she could tell her friends what a disaster it had been from start to finish. It could be her excuse never to have to do this again!

"Do you still want to do something?" she asked resignedly.

"I'd love to," he said. "But only if you don't mind?"

Jenna sat down and picked up a menu.

"Let's eat."

Two hours later, Jenna and Brad had only just left the café. Her mood had changed dramatically. Brad was funny, and smart and, once he'd finished apologising for the thousandth time, he was really very interesting. The fact that he was quite cute didn't hurt, either!

Illustration by
Bernie Dowling.

They'd decided to take a slow walk through the town, window shopping, just getting better acquainted, before meeting up with their friends. At the top of the shopping centre was the best ice-cream parlour in town. Jenna was amazed Brad had never eaten there and, deciding that she wouldn't mind seeing him again, took it upon herself to educate him in the way of all things cold and chocolatey.

They lingered at all the same shop windows, often interrupting each other in their haste to ask if the other minded going in. Jenna couldn't believe that what had started off as such a terrible date was now going so well. She had totally underestimated her friends this time — Brad was exactly what she needed.

Finally Brad reluctantly mentioned that it was probably time to make their way up to the cinema to meet their friends.

"I can't wait to tell Ryan what a great time I had today."

He slid his arm around Jenna's shoulders as he said it, and gently leaned in and kissed her softly on the head.

Jenna looked up at him. He really had beautiful eyes, she thought, closing hers and raising her head to meet his lips. Then she pulled away quickly.

"Who's Ryan?"

"Ryan. Ryan Black. Our mutual friend who set us up?"

"No." Jenna moved away slightly, shaking her head. "Penny Moore set us up."

"Who's Penny Moore?"

"You're kidding, right?"

Brad shook his head, concerned.

"You're not Brad Wilson, are you?" Jenna asked slowly.

"No, I'm Brad Morgan."

Jenna felt her jaw drop. She'd spent the day with the wrong guy! Suddenly it dawned on her. He hadn't used her name all day, and she'd never actually introduced herself. They'd just assumed . . .

"Who were you supposed to meet today?"

"Judy Greene. You're not her, are you?"

Jenna sighed, and she looked up at Brad. The best day she'd had in ages, certainly the best date she'd had, and it was with the wrong guy . . . or maybe not. A smile spread across her face and, as though it were contagious, Brad smiled. Then they laughed.

"What are the odds of two sets of people being set up to meet today, both at Café Olé?"

"We didn't meet at Café Olé," Jenna said through giggles. This got better by the second! "We met at the Old Café. Café Olé is two doors down."

THEY sat laughing for a while until Jenna thought of something.

"Your friends were meeting you tonight?"

"Yes, Ryan and his girlfriend."

"Well, your group just got bigger because I was meeting three of my friends and their partners."

"You still want to go?" Brad sounded horrified. "I mean, your date may not have turned up, but Ryan's going to be furious with me for standing this Judy girl up!"

Jenna stood up and reached for Brad's hand. He lifted himself from the seat and let himself be pulled towards her.

"Wasn't the whole point of setting you up today so that you could meet someone and be happy?"

Brad nodded.

"Then, didn't it work out that way anyway?"

Again the nodding. Jenna kissed him, for longer this time, and then dragged him back down towards the shopping centre.

At least it would be a great story to tell the grandchildren! ■

Picture This...

by Valerie Edwards.

H E'D stopped her just as she was popping a letter in the postbox by the school and, smiling, she'd turned round. Living on her own as she did, she liked to take the chance to stop for a chat whenever the opportunity arose.

Her morning walk to the shops took her past the children attending St Jude's in Bradley Road and there they all were, running into school, whooping and shouting.

She'd stand peering through the railings, envying the mothers more than anything.

It took her right back to the days of leaving her own daughters, Josie and Carrie, at the gates.

Josie had always loved to rush in without a single backward glance, but little Carrie had always hung back, lip trembling, not wanting to let go of the security of her mother's hand.

It was funny, Ruth thought now, how Josie had been the one to have all the confidence, all the verve and sparkle, and Carrie had been for ever in the background, shy and timid, with hardly a word to say for herself.

Illustration by
Bernard Dowling.

"She'll blossom, you'll see," Jack had said reassuringly, knowing she was

119

worried about their younger daughter. "She just feels — well, a bit overshadowed by her sister."

He'd been right, too, the way he usually was. When Josie had moved on to the big school — even though it was only next door to the Infants — Carrie had come out of her shell at last and she had seemed ready to face the world.

Both of them had done well, Ruth thought now, with a glow of pride. And she had good reason to be proud of her family, and she wasn't afraid to show it — but she did wish that Jack could be here to share it all with her.

But they'd had so many good times, she always made herself remember that. Just the four of them — well, five, if she counted the old yellow Allegro which was Jack's special toy.

She'd always considered that old car to be part of the family because they had so much fun in it.

They loved to visit the great houses and gardens. She was an avid photographer with a little Box Brownie Jack had bought early on in their marriage, and she faithfully recorded every visit. She had several albums full of memories.

MOSTLY she remembered the long curving staircases, all gilt and red carpets, and the huge ancestral portraits on the walls, the beautifully painted faces, every tendril of long hair detailed and every tiny crease in the elegant dresses delicately portrayed.

Ruth always longed to touch these gorgeous works of art, to feel the paint beneath her fingers.

She'd often wondered what it would be like to be a sitter — but not the

CAERPHILLY cheese was first sold in the Welsh town of the same name. Here it's combined with bacon and leeks to make a modern variation of Welsh cakes for a tempting breakfast.

Caerphilly Leek and Bacon Welsh Cakes

Pre-heat oven to 350 deg. F., 180 deg. C., Gas Mark 4.

Put 1 tsp oil in a frying-pan, add 3 oz chopped streaky bacon and cook for 3 to 4 minutes or until pale golden. Add a chopped leek and cook for a further 2 minutes. Cool.

Sift 8 oz plain flour, 1 tsp baking powder and a pinch of salt into a large bowl and rub in 2 oz butter. Stir in 2 oz crumbled Caerphilly cheese and cooled leek and bacon mixture.

Beat two eggs and stir enough egg into flour mixture to make a soft dough. Lightly knead, then cut in half. Roll each half out to a 5-in round circle, then cut into quarters.

Place a griddle or heavy frying-pan over a medium to low heat. Add four Welsh cakes at a time and cook for 4 to 5 minutes or until the base is

golden. Turn over and cook for a further 3 to 4 minutes. Place on a baking tray. Cook remainder in the same way. Bake for 5 minutes.

Heat 2 tbs oil in a non-stick frying-pan, crack in four eggs and fry for 2 to 3 minutes or until cooked to your liking. Split warm Welsh cakes in half, spread with a little butter and serve with a fried egg and a fried tomato. **Serves 4.**

Recipe and photography courtesy of British Egg Information Service.

painter, though. She'd never aspired to that as she'd been hopeless at drawing at school. But what it would actually be like to be the focus of the artist's attention?

She knew from just gazing at the portraits that you didn't necessarily need to be beautiful to begin with — the talent of the painters could make you seem so.

Feeling a little silly, she'd once mentioned it to Jack, hoping he wouldn't laugh. And, dearest Jack, he hadn't.

He just said something she'd never forgotten. It had been really sweet of him. He didn't need a portrait of her, he'd said, because he'd *never* forget her face.

Ruth still felt that aching loneliness. It had been ten years now since Jack had passed on, but she thought about him every single day. And she knew that the girls — although both of them were married now — did, too. He'd been such a good father. Everyone had loved him.

She gave a huge sigh and made herself think of the portraits again. Just imagine having oneself painted! Would she be able to sit still long enough? Rheumatism had a bit of a nasty habit of gripping you at just the wrong moment.

She remembered a friend telling her of a make-over at a beauty salon when first her wrist and then her elbow had locked. Apart from the obvious discomfort, she said it had also been quite embarrassing, in front of all these young folk!

Well, anyway, Ruth thought, settling herself more comfortably into the armchair, she hadn't thought twice when he'd asked her by the postbox. She'd

121

been really, really pleased — quite overwhelmed, in fact.

After all these years, Ruth told herself gleefully, laughter bubbling up inside, now her dream was finally coming true. If only Jack had still been here to share her moment of — well — of glory. How pleased he would have been!

She looked across at the artist. Face absorbed, head bent, a lock of black hair falling over his forehead, she thought he was exactly as she'd imagined the artists of old to have looked, although she'd never actually seen pictures of them — Gainsborough, Rubens, Franz Hal.

He worked fast and confidently, filling Ruth with admiration as she watched.

I OUGHT to have put on a prettier dress, she told herself. Maybe even had my hair done. *That* would certainly have surprised Madame Cleo. Two hairdos in ten days! How silly I am, she thought. An old woman like me — I should know better!

Ruth knew that the artist hadn't asked her to sit for a portrait because she was a beauty — not an old lady like she was. But she couldn't help wondering how the picture would turn out.

She noticed that the scratching of the crayons had stopped.

"Oh, have you finished?" she asked. "May I see?"

He nodded, stood, up and stretched. He held out the picture and she, too, stood up and took it almost reverentially.

Ruth looked down. A blur of bright colours, what seemed like a hand just there, a bright blue eye in the top corner. And was that an ear? She wasn't sure.

There was certainly a deep purple sky and, below, a lovely pink sea. Or perhaps it was land? Or maybe even a whole field of pink campions?

"It's an abstract," she breathed.

"No," he said solemnly, shaking his head. "It's you, Gran."

She studied it again, one arm round his shoulders, her fingers brushing his dark hair.

"Of course it is, Ben," she said. "It's beautiful."

She beamed down at him. How clever he is, she thought fondly, to draw as well as this at only seven. What will he be doing, my dear grandson, twenty years on?

"You know, I feel like the queen," she told him. "And this is going over my mantelpiece for everyone to see. But first you must sign it, across the bottom. Then, in the future, everyone will know that I was the very first sitter for the famous Ben Trevelyan. The very first! Oh, how proud of you your grandad would have been!" ■

Illustration by
Richard Eraut.

by Sally Hilton.

Where The Heart Is

L OOKING around, Katherine thought it could almost have been the
nineteenth century. The little country church was decorated today
for Harvest Festival. Sheaves of golden corn were tied to the altar
rail. Great striped marrows, bunches of carrots and fat cabbages
were arranged to best advantage in front of the pulpit.

Jars of home-made jam gleamed with jewelled colours on the window-
ledges. A basket of speckled eggs and a fresh loaf lay by the font. Everything
was just as it might have been for the last hundred years.

But the thought of the old building's echo of the past didn't charm
Katherine; it depressed her.

She was sitting, waiting for the service to start, in the ancient church at the heart of the small Wiltshire village where she now lived. It was one of four churches which her husband, Richard, had just taken on in his role as the new vicar.

Katherine hadn't really wanted to come here; the countryside was all right for day trips, she felt, but she was a town girl at heart.

She'd liked their previous appointment in a pleasant, suburban parish where the superstore was less than a mile away, and all sorts of amenities were right on the doorstep.

NOW here they were in the back of beyond, she thought bitterly, where you had to get in the car just to buy a pint of milk.

She'd have nothing in common with the people here, she'd decided. Most of them were farmers and they talked about things she didn't understand: tractors and milk quotas and lambing.

So far, there wasn't anyone she'd been able to chat to in a relaxed way. People were polite and kindly, but somehow they were always distant and reserved, a bit stiff and formal.

Katherine thought longingly of her friends in the old parish, so many miles away now, and of the good times and giggles they'd had together. She felt alone and out of place.

Richard had urged her to give the new place a chance, but it was different for him. His diary was packed with committees and speaking engagements. He was busy dashing about meeting people and getting to know the area. He had a ready-made role to step into.

Katherine hadn't managed to find a job yet and, at the moment, the days seemed long and empty.

And now here she was, back in the nineteenth century! Even the damp hymnbook that she'd been given on her way in seemed to belong to another age; its curling pages revealed nothing written since 1902. Only the organ marred the old-fashioned picture.

Richard had told her what had happened.

Apparently the old organ had finally given up the ghost only a week ago, having accompanied the congregation for a good century or so.

Arrangements for a proper replacement not having been made yet, someone had kindly loaned a modern electric keyboard. Mrs Chilcott, the church organist, had balked at this initially but, seeing no alternative, had resigned herself to it.

Now, for the first week, she sat at the new keyboard, ready to play the harvest hymns. She played a few background pieces as the congregation gathered.

People trooped in. There were elderly couples and young families; a real mix of ages. There was one woman in particular whom Katherine noticed; she was wearing a cheerful red beret and matching scarf. She was about Katherine's age, with a man who seemed to be her husband, and like Katherine and Richard, they had no children.

The woman gave Katherine a smile, and sat with her husband in the pew opposite. Others also smiled or nodded at Katherine, but nobody spoke, or came to sit next to her. When the service started, she was still sitting on her own.

As Richard climbed into the pulpit for the very first time, Katherine could tell he was nervous.

"Well," he began with a smile, "it's marvellous to be with you, and especially good to begin my time with you by celebrating the Harvest Festival today.

"I must say, the display is looking absolutely wonderful, and I'm sure that a lot of hard work has gone into it. I'd like to say a big thank you today to all the volunteers.

"And now, let's begin the service as we sing our first hymn, 'We Plough The Fields And Scatter'."

It was a big occasion for Richard; his first service at one of his new churches. He was a bit tongue tied, and rather pink around the ears, but generally managing very well, Katherine thought.

They all stood up to sing the hymn, which her neighbours bellowed out with great gusto and obvious enjoyment.

Richard settled into the service, guided everyone smoothly through prayers and Bible readings, and gave an appropriate sermon, which he had carefully made sure would not be too long.

Soon it was time for the last hymn. Richard announced, "All Things Bright And Beautiful". Mrs Chilcott launched into it enthusiastically on the electric keyboard, and the congregation joined in.

THEN, towards the end of the first verse, something happened. All of a sudden, a loud disco beat started up; drums pulsated rhythmically in a very odd accompaniment to the familiar tune.

Katherine looked up, startled. Mrs Chilcott must have accidentally knocked a switch and was frantically pushing and pulling switches to turn the beat off, but to no avail.

Nobody knew quite what to do. Richard was looking concerned and even pinker than before. It was impossible to ignore the thumping and its curious combination with the hymn.

Then Katherine saw the woman in the red beret and her husband look at each other and smile. They saw Katherine had noticed, and grinned at her, too. Behind her, Katherine heard some children laughing.

It was infectious; soon, the whole congregation was enjoying the joke, looking around at each other delightedly. Mrs Chilcott didn't mind. She had no idea what she'd done to start off this noisy intrusion, so she certainly didn't know what to do to stop it. With a wry grin and a shrug, she soldiered on.

And so it was that "All Things Bright And Beautiful" was sung to the accompaniment not only of a most peculiar drum beat, but of laughter, merriment and smiles.

KATHERINE felt her spirits rising. It seemed that Oxley was quite able to take the twenty-first century in its stride. What was more, these were people who might be a little shy to begin with, but who had a sense of fun, who could laugh at themselves, who could cope with the unexpected. She looked around again at the stained-glass windows with their timeless harvest display, and the happy faces, and she felt that, after all, this might be a good place to be.

Richard pronounced the blessing. The service was finished. Over the bowed heads, he indicated to Katherine that, as they had previously arranged, she should join him at the door to greet the parishioners on their way out.

Katherine got up from her seat with a lot less trepidation than she would have had only minutes before, but still, she was slightly anxious. What would things be like now, she wondered? What would people say? Were they glad to have a new vicar, or not?

She walked up to Richard, who smiled at her and squeezed her hand. Nervously, she stood next to him, watching for the first person to come out. They didn't have long to wait. Mrs Chilcott had abandoned her post at the recalcitrant keyboard and fell upon them with exclamations.

"Oh, Vicar, I don't know what to say . . . what will you think of us! And you, my dear," she turned to Katherine, "I should think you've never been to a harvest festival like this before! But welcome, anyway, welcome — we're so glad to have you — if only you can cope with us!"

Katherine laughed and assured her that she thought she could. Many others followed, joking and smiling, relaxed now the ice had been broken. They pumped Richard and Katherine's hands and bid them welcome.

Almost the last to leave were the woman in the red beret and her husband. They had hung back to let the others go out before them.

"Hello," she said. "You two must be good for us — everybody's saying what a great service it's been! I'm Jane and this is my husband, Steve.

"We're neighbours of yours, actually — we live on the same road as the vicarage. Perhaps you'd like to come round later this afternoon for coffee and a chat?"

"That would be great," Katherine replied. "It will be nice to get to know some of the neighbours!"

Yes, she thought, it was going to be fine here, after all. In fact, it was going to be fun. ■

by Sheila
Aird.

Illustration by André Leonard.

Dressed
For Success

AROUND the beginning of October, Amy came home from
Brownies all excited.

"We're having a Hallowe'en Party in three weeks' time!" she
announced. "There's going to be sausage rolls and crisps and juice
and we're all going to get dressed up."

As Amy chattered on I got the very clear impression that Brown Owl, a
lovely, super-efficient mum to three teenage girls, would be providing the
dressing-up clothes which the Brownies would wear as Hallowe'en outfits.

I didn't realise I had to be involved until next morning when we were
having breakfast and Amy mentioned the special prize.

127

"Emily Simpkins says *she's* going to win it. So we'll need to think of something really cool for me to wear."

"Prize?" I asked. "What kind of prize?"

"Oh, Brown Owl hasn't told us. She just said there would be one — something special for the best costume. So, what will I go as?"

I thought for a moment, taken by surprise.

"The supermarket has some . . ." I stopped in mid-sentence, silenced by Amy's horrified look.

"We can't buy a dressing-up outfit from the *supermarket*," she said, sounding as scandalised as if I had suggested stealing it. "That would be cheating. Brown Owl says we've got to use our imaginations. We've got to make our costumes from bits and pieces."

She pursed her mouth and looked thoughtful as she toyed with her cornflakes.

"We've got to find out what Emily Simpkins is going as." She looked up at me. "Her mum's a teacher, you know."

"She would be," I muttered darkly.

TEACHERS have access to all kinds of junk. Emily's mum would be able to produce a designer Hallowe'en costume from bits and pieces without blinking.

"Emily Simpkins's sister won the prize last year." Amy sighed. "She's in the Guides now."

I tried to think positive as I chewed my bottom lip. Amy would be mortified if another Simpkins carried off the special prize — whatever it was.

"Cleaners are every bit as good as teachers," I said, with a confidence I didn't feel. "We'll just need to think of something a little bit different."

"Cool." Amy grinned. Her faith in me was touching.

Sometimes Amy's a bit too much like her father. Daniel thought my middle name was Superwoman, too.

When Amy arrived a year after we were wed, Daniel was thrilled — until I told him my home cleaning service which had kept us fed and clothed since he'd become a full-time writer would need to be put on hold.

"I'll find a job," he said bravely. "We'll be OK."

To be fair, he did find a job — in a DIY store. But he wasn't cut out to give folk advice on how to do it themselves. He stuck it for six months until I went back to work.

Then the reality of fatherhood hit him like a steamroller. He simply wasn't cut out to be a house-husband, he said.

By the time Amy was two years old, he was with a bright young accountant who thought his writing should be encouraged at any price. Five years on, she hasn't changed her mind.

Being a one-parent family, I have nobody to discuss my worries with, so I take them to work with me. I've solved many a problem while polishing furniture and cleaning paintwork.

That morning I was still preoccupied with Hallowe'en costumes when I let myself into James Colman's flat in Cherrybank Court.

FOR the past year I've cleaned James's flat on the second and fourth Wednesdays of each month. Considering he's the untidiest man on the planet, most of my mornings are spent putting his possessions back where they belong.

Usually he's ready to leave for work when I arrive so, unless he's running early, we just exchange a few words. So I was surprised when I found him in the kitchen on his knees mopping up the contents of a jar of pickles.

He looked up.

"Sorry about the mess, Megan. I knocked the jar off the worktop."

It occurred to me that pickles for breakfast was rather an unusual choice.

"Accidents will happen." I shrugged kindly. "You get off. I'll clear up."

"If you're sure." He stood up and glanced at his watch. "I have to see a client in Clovenford and I'm late."

"Perhaps you should — er — change before you leave?" I removed a piece of gherkin gently from his left knee. "The smell is inclined to linger . . ."

James groaned.

"This is all I need." He pulled off his tie as he escaped to his bedroom.

By the time he reappeared wearing a dark navy suit and pale blue shirt I'd removed the broken pickle jar and its contents and mopped the floor clean.

"Has it gone — the smell, I mean?"

"Completely," I assured him. "You look fine."

In fact, he looked fabulous.

"That's the last time I'll attempt to clear out a kitchen cupboard," he said as he picked up his car keys. "Thanks, Megan!"

His gratitude was touching.

After he'd gone I tidied the kitchen and wiped the worktops. Then I decided to finish cleaning said cupboard, which housed James's stores.

To my surprise, inside it was absolutely immaculate. Every tin, jar and packet was in its rightful place. Frowning, I stared at it all. This was so unlike James!

Fortunately, in the living-room everything looked normal. I enjoy transforming an untidy room into a neat and shiny one. As I cleared spaces, dusted the skirting boards and vacuumed the carpet I focused my thoughts on Amy's Hallowe'en outfit.

What could she wear? Think of something original, I told myself. Everyone would be going as Catwoman, or a Powerpuff Girl, or Britney Spears — or whoever the latest teen idol was at the moment.

Call it instinct, but none of these said "Brownies" to me. I wanted something different.

The coffee table was home to three weeks' worth of old newspapers. I stacked them in a pile and moved them to the end of the table so that I could give it a good polish.

Think, Megan, think. I rubbed the table top until it shone. But by the time I'd finished cleaning James's flat I was no further forward.

SO have you thought of anything yet?" Amy asked that afternoon when I collected her from school.

"I've got a few ideas," I lied. "Just let me work on them."

Amy looked glum.

"I asked Emily what she'd be wearing but she said 'it's a secret'."

"I'll bet she hasn't decided yet." I forced myself to sound confident as I unlocked the car. "I'll just bet she hasn't a clue what to wear."

During the next two weeks, as I vacuumed carpets, polished furniture and washed down woodwork at different locations, I thought about Amy's costume. The longer it went on, the more desperate I became.

All was not well. I'd conjured up so many silly ideas my brain cells were quite weak. Even Britney Spears was beginning to look like a good option.

Then I hit on an amazingly simple solution.

On the fourth Wednesday in October I drove to Cherrybank Court again. The second I put my key in the lock James opened the door. I gasped in surprise. He was leaning on a pair of crutches.

One leg was plastered from his toes up to his knee. He was wearing a navy sweater, orange and yellow Bermuda shorts and one brown sandal on the unplastered foot.

"What happened?"

"Playing squash last Sunday. Damaged my Achilles tendon."

"It's easily done," I sympathised. "Is it very painful?"

"Agony." He winced bravely.

I followed him into the kitchen.

"Can I make you a cup of tea, or some toast, before I start?"

"The doctor says I should keep my strength up." He sat down carefully at the kitchen table and looked up at me humbly. "Breakfast would be nice."

I hadn't noticed before that his eyes were the colour of seaweed. They went nicely with his dark brown hair.

"I thought you didn't eat breakfast," I said as I dished up a full English.

Water-Magic

The breeze had blown the clouds away,
The sun was wide awake —
There never dawned a better day
For boating on the lake!

In picture-hats, with parasols,
The ladies lounged at ease;
Their escorts wielded oars or poles
And tried their best to please.

The snowy swans sailed proudly by
With dignity and grace,
Their beauty mirrored fleetingly
Upon the lake's calm face.

And happy voices rose and fell
In accents warm and gay,
As water wove its ancient spell
To drive all cares away.

No shadow dimmed the ripples bright,
And time stood still awhile,
That summer day, when hearts were light
And nature seemed to smile!
                    — Brenda G. Macrow.

"I don't when I'm rushing out to work. But today I'm not going anywhere and I feel in need of some comfort food." He forked a piece of bacon. "This is delicious, Megan. Thanks."

"I'll leave your crutches within reach," I said.

Eager to get started, I moved towards the door.

"If you need anything just shout."

I took my basket of polishes and dusters from the hall cupboard and went into the sitting-room — and stopped dead.

THE room looked immaculate. Everything was in its place. Every ornament, every photograph, every book was where it belonged. More to the point, the coffee table housed only one magazine and a coaster with a picture of the Eiffel Tower on it.

Dismayed, I sank down on to the sofa.

"Thanks for breakfast." James's voice cut into my thoughts. "I'll just sit for a while and take the weight off my leg."

I looked up at him.

"You had a pile of newspapers on this table two weeks ago."

"That's right. They were all ancient."

"I know." I forced myself to stay calm. "But what happened to them?"

"I threw them out."

"What?" I wailed. "You never throw anything out. You don't *do* tidy."

He looked surprised.

"Does it matter? I thought you'd be pleased." Embarrassed, he manoeuvred himself down beside me. "The room looked like a bomb site."

"It always does," I said, vexed beyond measure. I fumbled in my pocket for a handkerchief. "I make it tidy again. That's why you employ me. I *needed* those newspapers. I . . ."

Suddenly I realised James was staring at me in bewilderment. I was behaving like a woman obsessed.

"I'm sorry," I said stiffly.

His mouth twitched and his eyes twinkled like emeralds.

"It's not funny. My reputation is at stake here."

"I'm intrigued."

I explained as briefly as possible about the Hallowe'en party and the fact that Amy was counting on me to come up with a fantastic idea for a costume before next week.

"And the newspapers?"

"I thought she could go as a paper chase," I muttered. "I would have cut the newspapers into squares and attached them to her T-shirt with safety pins."

"I see." James looked thoughtful.

"OK. So it's a rotten idea but it's the best I could do. And now . . ."

It was all too much. Tears began to trickle down my cheeks.

"Don't, Megan. Please. This is all my fault." To my surprise he drew me into his arms. "If I hadn't tried to impress you by tidying up a bit myself, the newspapers would still be cluttering up the coffee table."

"Why did you want to impress me?"

He leaned back against the cushion and moved his plastered leg into a more comfortable position before answering.

"Because I think you're wonderful, beautiful, indispensable . . ." He paused. "And I look forward to the days of the month when you sort out my life."

"That's what cleaners do," I murmured.

"Oh, Megan, you're more than just my cleaner."

I smiled up at him.

"Really?"

Later, after I'd assured him that, although I was touched by his need to lessen my workload, I did truly enjoy transforming chaos into calm, we turned our thoughts to my big problem.

"When I was in the Cubs I won first prize at one Hallowe'en party," James mused. "I went as a scarecrow."

For an instant I was struck dumb.

"You're a genius," I said.

AMY looked absolutely fabulous dressed as a scarecrow. She wore my old jeans, tied with string, and a jacket belonging to James. I provided a cap, and James produced a multi-coloured scarf and gloves. I shredded a couple of yellow dusters into imitation straw to add an authentic touch and used blusher on Amy's cheeks to complete the look.

Pity she didn't win the prize — a beautifully illustrated book about animals. That went to a Brownie called Harriet. She turned up dressed as a pumpkin.

"She looked really cool, just like a real pumpkin," Amy said as I tucked her up in bed. "Her mum had dyed three pillow-cases bright orange and they were stuffed with lots of pillows. She had on a green pointy hat and her face was painted orange, too."

"At least Amy wasn't upset about not winning," James said later.

He sat in the corner of my sofa with his plastered leg stretched out in front of him on a low table. I was curled up comfortably in the crook of his arm.

"Yes, she was quite generous in defeat," I said proudly. "But I wonder how she would have reacted if Emily Simpkins had won?"

James's arm tightened round my shoulders.

"We would have coped," he said simply. ■

The Last Waltz

by Liz Gilbey.

WOULD you believe it? There I was, twirling round the dance floor like a youngster!

The band was playing the last waltz, my dancing partner was smiling broadly, and I felt happy and as light as a feather as I easily followed his steps. There was even a glitter ball shining high above us.

I could have been dreaming, of course. It was such a long time since I'd danced like this, or felt as happy and as relaxed as this, but I knew I wasn't dreaming.

How did I know? Because my granddaughter had just danced past me, caught my eye and winked at me conspiratorially.

"Enjoying yourself, Gran?"

Then she was whisked smoothly away by her young man, himself an expert dancer, suave and elegant in his blue pinstripe suit.

"You should know!" I called to her as she twirled away from me, and we grinned at each other.

I really was enjoying myself — and it was all thanks to my pretty granddaughter, Caitlin. With a little additional help from my dancing partner, of course. But mostly it was because of Caitlin, and a favour she could probably only ever have asked of her old gran.

Seven short weeks ago was the start of it all . . .

"You want me to show you how to do what?" I could hardly believe what Caitlin had just asked me as we sat in my kitchen, sharing tea and biscuits that Monday afternoon. She always called in on her way home from school, and I must say that I looked forward to her visits.

Her request today, however, was certainly not one I'd ever heard of a granddaughter asking her grandmother before!

"The jitterbug, Gran. Mum says she remembers seeing you and Grandad dancing it when she was small. She's never forgotten it!"

"Why do you want me to teach you how to do the jitterbug?" I had to ask, and she grinned, producing a poster out of her school haversack.

134

Illustration by
Patricia Ludlow.

"Because of this!" she said.

Get In The Mood For A 1940s Ball! screamed the bright red headlines of the poster. *Jitterbug the night away! A swinging evening for charity! 1940s dress positively encouraged!*

"Goodness," I said. "What a great idea!"

I can't pretend that the poster didn't take me back in time. Too young to take part in the war — I was only twelve when hostilities ended — the music and the clothes and everything from then always seemed so glamorous to me.

I taught myself all the latest dances from books in my bedroom, humming the tunes and dancing in that tiny space with my best friend, Mary.

"So will you teach me, Gran?"

Caitlin's repeated question brought me out of my trip down memory lane.

"But why do you want me to teach you to jitterbug?"

"I don't know how to do any proper dances, Gran. Simon Grainger will be there and my friend Cass says he knows how to jitterbug. His mum and dad dance — dance properly, I mean — and I . . ."

She went pink and her voice trailed off. She had had a crush on Simon Grainger for months, and I guessed that she didn't want to embarrass herself in front of him.

"Anyway, our next-door neighbour Carol is organising the ball. Remember, she organised that sponsored walk we went on last year? Mum says she can get us costumes from the drama society, too, so all I need to do is learn to dance!"

"Hmm. The jitterbug is really lots of dances, you know — Lindy Hop to rock and roll. But your biggest problem is finding someone to learn with; it's not a dance style you can learn alone, and I'm a bit past twirling you round my head . . ."

"No problem, Gran! Tim wants to learn, too. He just got me to do the asking!"

"Your poor twin gets roped in to all sorts of daft stunts." I laughed. "But I think you should learn to waltz as well, while we're at it. It'll be much more useful in the long run."

"You are the most wonderful gran ever!" She giggled and hugged me.

SO, twice a week, we pushed back the furniture in the dining-room of my bungalow and Caitlin, her twin brother Tim and I danced. We also laughed a lot, got completely out of breath, and generally had a high old time.

"Jitterbug started in 1934 when a musician called Edwin Swayzee wrote a song called 'The Jitterbug' for band leader and singer Cab Calloway," I explained.

It was a long time since I had taught anyone to dance. Yet George and I had loved dancing. We had met at a dance class, danced our way into love and marriage, and kept up the hobby throughout our lives.

We even taught the girls in our daughter Jane's Girl Guides how to dance for proficiency badges! That must be where Jane remembered seeing us jitterbug. Fancy that! The things your children remember from when they are small.

Since George died two years ago, I had more or less given up dancing. Well, to tell you the truth, I'd given up most things. It just wasn't the same, going on your own.

Everyone at the dance club or holiday tea dances were pleasant and friendly enough, but it wasn't the same. Going alone just brought back too many memories of the happy times we'd had together, as a couple. And it's easy enough to be sad, with so many reminders of the past.

You get out of the habit of going out after a while — out of the habit of bothering. And when there's no-one of your own to share things with, it's much easier to stay at home in the warm with a book or the TV for company,

136

not going to all the trouble of getting changed and going out. Then, after a bit, you forget how to make the effort, and why you should still bother.

That was the state I had got into without realising it. I had become a lonely old lady within her own four walls. Sometimes I saw no-one for days. Apart from the family, that was. And the milkman.

Being without George had knocked all the confidence out of me, I could see that now . . .

IT seemed very strange to be teaching someone to dance again. I had felt very nervous to begin with, but if you can't teach your own grandchildren, who can you teach?

And I was amazed how quickly it came back to me! I tried not to blind them with science. I just taught them the basics of dancing Swing, but avoided the acrobatics and intricacies of the Whip and the East Coast. After all, I wanted to encourage them, not put them off!

They enjoyed themselves and had natural aptitude, my teenage grandchildren. They even wanted to learn more. I was proud of them. Despite being at that gawky stage, they both had natural grace. So I did teach them to waltz — eventually. Just in case it might come in handy one day.

The night before the ball we had a bit of a party — a dress rehearsal really — at my bungalow. Caitlin and Tim, with their mum and dad, Jane and Derek, came and bopped the night away (well, an hour or so!) and stayed for supper. It was a lovely family evening, and all the nicer for being unexpected.

"Why don't you come to the ball with us, Mum?" Jane asked. "It's going to be a great night out. Carol's worked hard to get the details right. Everyone is wearing 1940s civilian and military dress."

"I'm going as a Canadian airman!" Tim told me proudly.

"There's a live band, a dancing display by a local night class, and even period food, if we're brave enough to eat it," my daughter continued.

"Oh, no!" I said, feeling sick suddenly. "I can't do that! I don't go out any more. I know it sounds lovely, but I've probably forgotten how to do all that sort of thing. And it's for you youngsters, really . . . You don't need your old granny tagging along."

I could hear myself running out of excuses, and I felt quite ashamed of myself when I saw their faces.

"Come on, Mum, you'll love it."

"You can't sit around moping for ever, you know."

"But you've got to come. We've told everyone about how our gran trips the light fantastic!"

"Grandad would have come if he'd been here — he'd have loved it."

That was Caitlin, of course. And suddenly I knew that she was right; they were all right. Loss was one thing, deep grief something else. But sitting and moping was quite another.

Then something extraordinary happened. I suddenly imagined my George, back there in his chair by the fire. I remembered how he would grin, his eyes lighting up, then laugh.

"Come on, my girl, let's get on to that dance floor and show the young 'uns how to do it!" he'd say.

So I didn't waste any more time thinking about it. It would be a real treat, I told myself firmly. And it would be lovely to be out together as a family — and we'd be helping a good cause. Yes, George would definitely have approved!

The "In The Mood 1940s Charity Ball" the next evening was at the school where both Tim and Caitlin were sixth formers. Banners and old wartime posters greeted us as we walked in. Jane and Derek were trim and smart, both wearing the Army uniforms they had last worn in an amateur dramatic society revue of Forties music.

Caitlin wore a soft blue dress — Airforce blue, of course — with padded shoulders, feature pockets and cuffs, and a neat little belt. She was beautiful. The outfit suited her complexion and her fair hair, and I hoped Simon Grainger was going to appreciate the effort she had made! Tim looked very handsome and elegant in his uniform, too.

Me? I wore something that used to be called a costume — a trim grey suit dress, slimming and formal, a design classic for any era. I'd given it a Forties look with a smart ladies' trilby, dressed up with a jaunty pheasant feather and a marcasite hat pin.

It was in the window of a charity shop, along with a pale grey blouse with outwork collar. So I bought both! And now, at the ball, I would become a demure, matronly lady, who might well have been running a school. Or a ration book office.

And there was another thing to commend my new formal look — I wasn't dressed for jitterbugging. I certainly wasn't going to get cajoled into that!

THE school hall was transformed. There was a wonderful atmosphere as people of all ages set out to celebrate the Forties. The food on offer included such delicacies as Woolton pie, war and peace pudding, Spam fritters and eggless sponge cake. It seemed everyone was sampling everything on the tables, and a happy wander down memory lane was had by all.

I was surprised to find I knew so many people, and managed to keep chatting — and dancing — all evening. I saw people I hadn't seen for years! It was great fun, and somehow the magic of a well-positioned hat pin kept my hat on my head, even though I could feel the feather waving about madly.

It was lovely to see old friends again, catch up with the gossip, remember

Pitlochry

THIS charming little Perthshire town came to prominence in Victorian times, thanks to the romantic novels of Sir Walter Scott and the approval of Queen Victoria.

The arrival of the railway in 1863 ensured it became one of the premier mountain resorts, while its central location makes it a perfect starting point to tour Scotland.

Nestled in the prettiest of scenery, Pitlochry has long been popular with tourists, who come to enjoy the many natural attractions, cultural events and excellent shops which flourish here.

J. CAMPBELL KERR.

the good old days. I was, I realised with something of a jolt, enjoying myself. I hoped George wouldn't mind, or feel that I was being disloyal.

But I knew he wouldn't. It was George who had always said I was too serious, too earnest, that I needed to enjoy myself, and to enjoy life more.

And then, when everyone changed dancing partners in a Paul Jones, I skipped sideways into the arms of a tallish, elegant man wearing a wonderful blue serge double-breasted suit.

"My stars! It's Lesley Ellis, isn't it? Armstrong as was?" he said, his rather pleasant brown eyes wrinkling into a heartwarming smile.

"Yes, it is," I replied a bit breathlessly. "But who . .?"

I looked again as he put his head slightly on one side, looked at me with mock seriousness, and laughed.

"I haven't changed that much, have I? You certainly haven't!"

And suddenly I knew who he was. The boy I had sat next to at infant school, whom I had grown up with, who had married Grace Morris from the next village, and moved away to London.

"John Bryant!" I said, amazed. "I don't think I've seen you for forty years or more! How are you?"

"I'm fine, Lesley, and delighted to see you. My son David encouraged me to come tonight; he thought I might see someone from the old days. And I've seen several people I used to know, but I'm thrilled to meet you again.

"Shall we sit this dance out, get a home-made lemonade and slice of eggless sponge, and catch up on old times?" he suggested gallantly.

AND that was what we did. He told me about his life and work in London, his family and how he had just returned to Westrill to live near his son and grandchildren since being widowed.

So I told him about George, and Jane, and Tim and Caitlin. And we laughed about the food, and our shared memories of growing up, and the forty-two years since we had last met seemed no time at all.

Perhaps I should not have been quite so amazed to see John again, I realised as we sat and chatted. His career had taken him away from our home town, and I knew from mutual friends that he had regularly returned to visit his family. What I hadn't realised — until John told me — was that those visits had encouraged John's son, David, to love the little market town. He was the one who had moved back with his family in the end.

In the same easy companionship of old, we watched the displays of Lindy Hop and jitterbug, reminisced about Saturday dances we had enjoyed in the brand-new War Memorial Hall, and sang along to old hit tunes played by the band. And then we danced again.

The last waltz came all too soon, and it was with that wonderful, powerful yet floating feeling that John and I matched steps and body movements as we swung gently round the floor.

"I'm glad this is a waltz," John murmured into my hair. "I don't think I'm up to doing the jitterbug any more. My muscles would ache for days afterwards!"

WE laughed then, and it was more than delightful to see the twinkle in his eyes as we shared the joke.

"Enjoying yourself, Gran?" a voice by my side asked.

Caitlin waltzed serenely past in the arms of Simon Grainger. They looked a perfectly matched couple, and Simon was smiling very sweetly at her.

"You should know!" I called to her and I could hear the laughter in my voice.

"That's my granddaughter, Caitlin," I explained proudly to John, and he nodded and smiled to Caitlin and Simon.

"She's very pretty," John said. "No wonder you're so proud of her."

"Oh, it's not just being proud of her that's making me smile," I said. "I'll let you in on a secret — I've only just taught her to waltz! She was determined to learn the jitterbug, but I insisted she learn to waltz as well. And I think," I added, a bit mischievously, "she's getting more fun from waltzing!"

"I get a lot of fun from waltzing, too," John said, smiling back at me. "We dance well together, Lesley, even after all these years! Why don't we do it again, some time soon? I haven't wanted to go out much since I lost Grace, and we would both enjoy catching up on old times. What do you think?"

"That would be marvellous, John. Thank you!"

The years between us dropped away as I remembered the grave, well-behaved little boy with the wicked grin that had been John. I daresay he remembered the chatterbox with the wonky hair ribbon that had been me, too! We had been very different in those days, but we had shared friendship, secrets, ambitions and much laughter.

Life had parted us, but here we were, brought together again unexpectedly, finding the old friendship had endured. And I also thought George would have approved, seeing me smiling and chatting, enjoying meeting old friends like I used to. And dancing again.

"There's just one thing, though," I said soberly.

"What's that?"

"I must teach Caitlin to tango," I explained, seeing my granddaughter and Simon deep in conversation, heads close together, both of them smiling, holding each other close. "And you can help me!"

"What? Teach the tango?" He thought about it and then nodded.

"Tango, paso doble, polka, you name it!" He laughed, and his laughter was infectious. "Lead on, Ginger, I'm more than willing to be your Fred Astaire!" ■

Hidden Talents

by Gwen Barnes.

W E were clearing out the attic of my uncle's old house when I came across the portrait.

"Who is this?" I asked my mother and she looked at it in puzzlement for a moment.

"Oh, that must be your father's grandmother," she said, enlightenment dawning. "I never knew her. She died young."

"So now I know who to blame." I grinned, examining the dark-haired girl in the picture. It explained why I was the odd one out in my family.

My family were brilliant. I don't just mean that we all got on very well and were genuinely fond of each other — that was brilliant, of course, because you hear of families who do nothing but quarrel.

But I mean *they* were *brilliant.* My father was a manager. My mother was a maths teacher. My younger sister was at university reading something impossibly complicated. My elder brother was one of these fabulous computer whiz-kids.

Me? Now that was the problem. I was just ordinary at school. I was never good at sports. I wasn't musical. I wasn't particularly good at anything. I was even between jobs at the time.

As for looks — well, all the rest of them were tall, willowy and handsome. My sister was the most gorgeous blonde with beautiful long legs. I was ordinary, small, five-foot nothing, with dark hair which always went its own way, no matter what I tried to do with it, and a little snub nose. Somewhere along the line I had missed out.

Now the mystery was solved. It was Great-grandmother who'd passed her genes on to me.

"What was she like?" I asked Mum.

"I really don't know, dear. I think her name was Daisy, but I don't remember hearing very much about her and there's no-one who'll remember now, I'm afraid."

I studied the face of the young girl who looked so like me. She might have been pretty — it's always difficult to tell with stiff old portraits.

"You must have been good at something," I murmured. "What was it? Something good you could have passed on to me? After all, I've got your nose and your hair."

Illustration by Bianchi.

But the portrait wasn't telling.

There was the usual lot of old rubbish in the attic — dusty lampshades, things that no longer worked, mismatched china, boxes of old tatty books.

Mum made me check each one in case there were any valuable first editions, but there weren't, of course. At the bottom of the last box, however, was a dusty little red book, very worn at the edges. I was all set to sling it in the rubbish pile when something made me open it — and when I turned the first page I felt a queer little thrill.

Daisy Morris — Her Book, I read. Now I might find out something about her, my look-alike relative!

No such luck. There were no revelations, just a lot of notes about housekeeping and recipes that would help a young housewife of the time.

There were occasional remarks in her beautifully neat script, like *Got feet wet in the rain but Aunt Maggie's recipe for toddy was excellent.* Or, *This cream is wonderful for my freckles.*

My eye was caught by *Aunt Maggie's cakes — my dear husband's favourites.* I read the recipe with interest.

I might try that some time, I thought.

It wasn't that I was a particularly good cook, it was just that with all the others so involved with their interests and papers everywhere, it fell to me to make a lot of the meals.

But of course, it soon went quite out of my mind.

* * * *

"Oh, Vicky, do you think you could make me some cakes for the school fête?" Mum asked me a couple of months later. "I promised we'd contribute something. How about trying something a bit different from the usual sponges and gingerbread this year?"

It was then that I remembered Aunt Maggie's recipe and decided to try it out. I had to shop for a few of the ingredients, but the delicious aroma when the cakes were cooking made my mouth water. My brother came in as the first batch was cooling, and he snaffled one before I could stop him.

"Mmm. These are delicious. I could eat a dozen."

"Oh, no, you don't!" I scolded. "They're for Mum's fête."

With a struggle, I managed to push him out of the kitchen and shut the door on him. I packed the cakes into boxes before he could steal any more.

The fête came and went, and I forgot about them.

SO it was a considerable surprise, one morning a few days later, when I answered a knock at the door to find a young man standing on the doorstep with one of my boxes in his hand.

"I'm sorry to bother you, but I'm looking for Mrs Morris."

"That's my mother, but she's not home at the moment. Can I help you?" He looked rather nice and I was hoping I could.

"It's about these cakes . . ."

My heart sank like a stone.

"Oh, dear — was something wrong? I hope no-one's been ill or anything. I made them." I had a moment's terrible panic. It had, after all, been an unusual recipe.

"No, no, it's nothing like that. It's just that they were especially good and most unusual. I wondered if there was any way you could let me have a copy of the recipe?"

"Why?" This was unexpected — not many men had ever asked me for a recipe.

"Well, actually . . ." He looked a bit embarrassed. "My mother and I run a cake shop and we're always looking for something a bit different. I can see our customers taking to these in a big way!"

I was flattered, but still inclined to be wary.

"It's — er — my great-grandmother's secret recipe," I explained. "I'm not sure if I want to give it away."

That might have been the end of our acquaintance, nipped in the bud before it even began, but just then Mum came up the garden path.

"Where are your manners, Vicky, keeping your friend on the doorstep? Go in, both of you — and put the kettle on, there's a dear. I'm gasping for a cup of tea."

Before I could say that he wasn't a friend but a complete stranger, she'd ushered us indoors.

"Well, you'd better sit down," I said to him, embarrassed. "Would you rather have tea or coffee?"

Then it was introductions all round and explanations. His name was David and he was really quite nice. The upshot of it was that he invited me over to his shop in the next town, where I met his mother.

It turned out that David acted as manager, dealing with the accounts and the business side mainly — but he enjoyed doing the occasional spot of cooking as well.

OF course, I made some of Aunt Maggie's cakes for them to sell, and they were a great success. They sold like — well, like hot cakes! David's mother was a good cook, far better than me, but she often needed extra help, and when things were hectic I lent a hand — and would you believe it, I discovered I did have a talent after all.

It turned out that I had a very steady hand and endless patience, and a bit of an artist's eye, so when it came to decorating cakes and making those beautiful little sugar flowers and medallions, I was in my element. I even invented a few new styles.

I recalled that I used to doodle tiny detailed pictures in my schoolbooks, so I dug them all out to have another look at them. Actually, looking at them again after all these years, they were much better than I remembered.

With David's encouragement, I took lessons and, through time, I became a real expert. I was a brilliant miniature artist, David said proudly.

In due course, I have to say, we made a very good partnership, David, his mother and I — and David and I in particular.

One very odd thing happened as we unpacked the last few boxes after our honeymoon. I had kept the portrait of Great-grandmother Daisy and as I unwrapped it, the frame fell to pieces.

We examined it carefully and, on the back of the canvas picture, we found there were lots of beautiful little paintings of flowers, tiny and detailed, around the words *Daisy — Her Work*. A miniature artist! So I had inherited more than just her nose and hair.

It was a nice feeling — as if I belonged at last. ■

Made For Each Other

by Christine McKerrell.

“COME along, Muffin, old girl.” Louisa Birket turned from the gate and made her cautious way to the back door of Twin Gables.

“Not the weather for either of us to be out in over long, is it?”

Louisa, or Lulu as her friends called her, paused to use the boot scraper by the kitchen door before stepping inside. From the direction of the parlour, Major Jimson wandered through to the kitchen, drink in hand.

“Old girl comfortable now, is she?” he enquired.

His hostess nodded.

“I suppose the way one views the first snowfall of winter rather depends on one’s age.”

Louisa made a wry grimace.

"Yes," she agreed. "Where youngsters see lots of fun with snowball fights and sledge rides, we old fuddy duddies think only about the cold and inconvenience."

The major huffed in reply.

"You an old fuddy duddy? Never!"

Louisa Birket had lived in the village of Blessenby all her adult life. Arthur Birket had brought her there as a bride and left her there a widow.

Not one to dwell unnecessarily on the past, and brought up to make the best of all life sent her way, Louisa threw herself into single life with the same enthusiasm she'd brought to her marriage. There was scarcely a society or a good cause in the county that did not have Louisa Birket on its committee.

Sausages and Stilton Mash

STILTON is often referred to as the "King" of English cheeses. The name comes from the village in Cambridgeshire where the cheese was originally traded in the early eighteenth century. Ironically, Stilton has never been made in Stilton village.

Peel and quarter 2 lb of potatoes. Cover with cold water, bring to the boil and cook for 20 to 25 minutes until they begin to fall apart. Drain the potatoes, leaving a little of the cooking water in pan.

Mash potatoes until there are no lumps, then stir in 6 fl oz milk. Mix in 2 oz walnuts and crumble in 4 oz Stilton cheese. Season to taste with pepper and nutmeg. Adjust consistency with milk to suit your taste. Serve with sausages. **Serves 4.**

Recipe developed by Stilton Cheese Makers Association in conjunction with the National Osteoporosis Society.

Carmichael is no longer with us. He tossed off scripts with no more thought than he gave to his sermons."

The young man grinned.

"I rather envy Mr Carmichael his literary bent. I'm afraid I spend the whole week agonising over my sermon. As for writing for the stage, that's well beyond my capabilities, I fear."

Louisa's smile was reassuring.

"Then why don't you allow me to help? I typed everything up for the late reverend, you know. Some of it must have rubbed off, I'm sure."

Peter Lewis's face cleared for a moment and then he frowned.

"But is there time?" he wondered.

"Ten weeks? Oh, I think so."

YOU'VE offered to do what?" The major chortled when he called at Twin Gables later that day.

Louisa peered sternly at her visitor over the rim of her spectacles.

"No need to sound so astonished," she said. "I am published, you know."

"In the parish magazine!" The major hooted. "Hardly Wordsworth, is it?"

"How fortunate our dear vicar thinks differently then," she told him, "since I've promised to come up with some ideas this very evening."

"Lulu, old girl, nobody appreciates your capabilities more than I, but this

150

DRIED plums, or prunes, were popular in mediaeval times, but gradually, in the sixteenth and seventeenth centuries, they were replaced by raisins. Dishes such as plum pudding and plum cake eventually used raisins but continued to be called "plum" in honour of the original ingredients. During the Puritan years, plum pudding was outlawed for being "sinfully rich"!

Plum Puddings

Lightly grease six individual pudding bowls. Put one small, chopped orange into a food processor and whizz until a pulp. Set to one side.

In a large mixing bowl, beat together 3 oz butter and 2 oz molasses sugar until light and fluffy. Add an egg, and 1 oz plain flour, ½ tsp each ground cinnamon and nutmeg, 4 oz fresh white breadcrumbs, 2 tbs brandy and 4 oz each of chopped prunes and seedless raisins. Combine thoroughly, stirring in orange pulp.

Spoon into pudding bowls and top each tightly with aluminium foil. Steam puddings for 45 minutes. Remove puddings and leave to stand for 10 to 15 minutes, before turning out. Serve with custard.

Makes 6 puddings.

Recipe courtesy of Lesley Waters for Julian Graves.

evening? Are you sure?"

His companion gave a gracious nod of the head.

"They are invited for drinks at eight. You may join us if you've nothing better to do."

"They, you say?"

Louisa turned a look of sublime innocence on her old friend.

"It was suggested we call on the expertise of a specialist in view of the limited time available."

"It was suggested?"

"Well, I suggested it, actually."

"And this expert is?"

Louisa turned her attention to shuffling the sheets of paper, as yet pristine and unsullied, on Arthur's desk.

"A pantomime does need music, Lionel."

The major groaned aloud.

"I thought so! It will likely end in tears, you know."

It's surprising how easily even the oldest of friends can suffer a falling out. Harsh words such as "meddlesome old busybody" and "dreary old fuddy duddy" were exchanged in the heat of the moment.

Lionel did not, on this occasion, stay for his usual drink, nor did he join the drinks party later that evening.

The meeting had gone splendidly, Louisa considered, as she saw her guests to the door. Anna really was a delightful girl, and the vicar such a gentleman. A smile tweaked at Louisa's lips as she waved the pair off.

Peter Lewis had shown remarkable restraint throughout, but young Anna Sudberry had struggled to bite her tongue on several occasions!

"These are just a few hastily gathered ideas, you understand," Louisa had been at pains to assure them. "But I rather thought we should try something a little more 'with it', as I believe they say, this year. The late reverend, bless him, was something of a dyed-in-the-wool traditionalist."

Her guests had nodded dutifully, though Peter had felt driven to defend his predecessor.

"Not that there's anything wrong with tradition, Lulu." He had smiled. "The church would be all the poorer without it."

"And people do rather enjoy knowing what to expect," Anna added. "It's all part of the fun."

Louisa waved away their concerns and insisted on pouring them all another drink.

AS she did the honours she caught the look of consternation that passed between the pair and smiled to herself.

"Now," she said, adopting a business-like tone, "what do you say to Cinderella?"

Her guests nodded in unison. This was clearly a good start. Louisa drew breath.

"But our Cinders should be a thoroughly modern miss. None of this sweeping out the ashes lark. After all, how many of our schoolchildren have actually seen an open fire these days? And, rather than a hackneyed old ball, I thought there should be one of those rave thingamajigs that are always being mentioned on the news."

"But what," Anna muttered faintly when at last Louisa paused for breath, "about the fairy godmother? There's always a fairy godmother."

"Precisely!" their hostess crowed. "So we will have a fairy godfather. Equality of the sexes and all that!"

"And Prince Charming?"

"Yes," Louisa mused. "I suppose that we can't avoid that, though perhaps he could be one of those rock stars."

"Well." Peter nodded, somewhat at a loss. "You've certainly given us something to think about . . ."

Their hostess beamed.

"Good! I'm sure the two of you can put your heads together and come up with something really splendid."

As Louisa saw the pair off, Muffin padded to her side.

"Well, old girl," her mistress said softly as she watched Peter and Anna stride off down the lane deep in conversation. "That's put the cat nicely amongst the pigeons."

W HATEVER are we to do?" Anna was asking.
Peter shrugged.
"I really don't know," he admitted. "She seems so keen on the idea." He drew in his breath. "I suppose it might just work."

His companion shook her head.

"Not in this neck of the woods. They want ugly sisters and 'Look behind you!' at every turn."

Peter Lewis chuckled.

"So do I," he confessed as they turned together to give a final wave. "But where do we start?"

"I could pop round tomorrow evening. Perhaps we could thrash out a compromise," Anna offered.

Peter threw her a look of gratitude.

"That would be wonderful," he agreed.

Witnessing the exchange, Louisa allowed herself a moment of smug satisfaction. No matter what the wretched Lionel said, they made a delightful couple . . .

*   *   *   *

As the weeks drew on, Louisa began to find the evenings spent alone, with only Muffin for company, somewhat tedious. She was fast discovering that she missed the old fool more than she could ever have imagined.

Though he bobbed his cap politely whenever they met in the village, and enquired most assiduously after her health, no longer did he share her pew in church or surreptitiously pass the bag of extra strong mints as they settled down to listen to the sermon. Nor did he wander in hopefully after his morning stroll to see if she had the kettle on the boil.

The parlour seemed most peculiarly empty without him and even old Muffin appeared to miss a man's presence about the place.

"Drat and double drat!" Louisa said aloud, one evening. "Never mind you, old girl. I miss a man about the place!"

Her sole consolation, small though it was in light of Lionel's desertion, was that Anna Sudberry and the vicar appeared to be getting on extremely well.

"Do you think Mrs Birket minded very much?" Anna had asked Peter one evening at rehearsals. "I mean, we hardly took her suggestions to heart."

The vicar of St Bede's smiled at his co-conspirator and she felt a warm glow colour her cheeks.

Peter Lewis was simply the sweetest man she'd ever known. If Mrs Birket hadn't come up with her outlandish ideas, they might never have got together.

"Do you know," he was saying now, "I don't think she cared one jot."

"It's a pity she couldn't be persuaded to take part." Anna sighed. "She's been a bit down lately, I think."

"Oh?" Peter asked, concern in his voice. "Nothing serious, I hope?"

His companion shrugged.

"A falling out is what I heard."

"Ah." Peter nodded. "The major. Yes, I thought I hadn't seen the pair of them lately. Shame he didn't want anything to do with the show either. It might have brought them together again."

Anna Sudberry beamed at him.

"Peter, you're a genius!"

"I am?"

"If we didn't have half the village watching our every move I'd kiss you."

Peter Lewis lowered his voice to a whisper.

"There's always later," he murmured. "The boys are expecting you back for supper. The pair of them are hoping for another chapter of 'The Hobbit'."

"They're super kids," Anna told him. "I was afraid they might resent me."

Peter shook his head.

"Not a bit of it. They think their old man needs taking in hand."

Anna nodded.

"As do another pair I can think of."

"Lulu and the major? What's the story there?"

"Lionel Jimson was best man at the Birkets' wedding."

"Never married himself?"

Anna shook her head.

"Rumour has it he fell head over heels in love with Louisa the minute he saw her and has carried a torch ever since."

"'Until now."

"Mm," Anna mused. "I can't understand what's happened to change things."

"But you have an idea about how to put it right . . ."

ON the night of the dress rehearsal Louisa arrived early at the village hall.

"We really could do with your help, Lulu," the vicar had pleaded. "Half of them don't know their lines, while the other half make it up as they go along."

He hadn't been totally convinced it was proper for a man of the cloth to

Blackberry Fun

Ringlets bobbing, ribbons flying,
Bonnets cast aside —
Lassies dancing down a lane,
Go singing, merry-eyed;
A small boy in a sailor-suit
Comes tottering after, plump and cute,
And soon they find the sweetest fruit
The hedgerow can provide.

Mother, following, sets a picnic
Underneath a tree;
The children joyful, blackberry-picking,
View the sight with glee;
As they find each juicy berry,
Purple lips reveal the story!
All the family making merry
When it's time for tea!

— *Maggie Smith.*

indulge in falsehoods till Anna pointed out that wasn't entirely the case. They did indeed need all the help they could get.

The call Anna Sudberry made to the major was very much along the same lines.

"My dear girl, I'd be delighted," he had promised, glad of any excuse to escape the resounding silence of his own living-room.

The lights had just gone down and the first scene was underway when Lionel Jimson shuffled through the dimly lit hall and fumbled his way to the vacant chair next to Louisa.

She turned and frowned at the intrusion.

"What are you doing here?" she demanded frostily.

"I could ask the same of you," the major blustered in return. "I'm here at the express request of a young lady."

"It was the vicar himself who asked me," Louisa told him in no uncertain terms, brandishing her script.

"I'm the prompt."

In reply Lionel held up his own copy of Cinderella.

"Me, too." His brows furrowed and then a smile began to twitch at the corners of his mouth.

"Do you know," he chuckled, "if I didn't know better I'd say we'd been set up!"

Louisa gave him an old-fashioned look.

"Don't be ridiculous," she told him.

Lionel cocked his head to one side.

"Is it so very ridiculous," he mused, "that someone should think we might enjoy one another's company?" There was a wistful note in the major's voice that a woman couldn't miss.

"Of course not, you silly old duffer," she muttered. "The vicar makes a splendid Prince Charming, does he not?" she said archly, to cover her confusion.

"And Miss Sudberry a glorious Cinders," her companion ventured. "Made for each other, I'd say."

Louisa smiled at him through the gloom.

"You really think so?"

"Indubitably."

On a sudden impulse that quite took the major's breath away, Louisa leaned across and planted a kiss on his cheek.

"Pax?" she ventured hesitantly.

Lionel reached out to give her hand a squeeze and quite forgot to let it go.

"Oh, yes, old girl," he agreed, his voice suddenly and inexplicably gruff. "Most definitely pax . . ." ■

The Christmas Gift

by Judith Davis.

Illustration by Melvyn Warren-Smith.

HANNAH CORKHILL waved importantly as the train drew out of Ramsey station. Her father, Mick, gradually receded until he looked no bigger than a doll, and the station buildings something she could have bought from a toyshop.

Hannah tugged energetically on the thick leather strap to close the window, then plumped back on to the cushioned seat, beaming.

She felt so full of excitement that her breakfast toast refused to settle. Here

157

she was, on her way to Douglas town, on the day before Christmas Eve!

It would have been grand to be going all that way alone. That would have been really exciting, but Grandma would be joining her at Sulby, two stops along the line. Until then, she could pretend she was a great lady, off to do her Christmas shopping in the metropolis.

With aloof deliberation, Hannah undid the ties on her hat and removed it. Mother had said to take her hat and gloves off on the train, and loosen her coat, otherwise she might feel cold when she reached her destination. Hannah did this, bowing to right and left, just as she imagined a great lady might.

Then she forgot her pretence, because the train had almost reached the inkpot-shaped house, and she *had* to look out at it, crossing her fingers at the same time. If she didn't see the inkpot house on her way out of Ramsey, she always felt she might have bad luck.

SHE couldn't risk bad luck today. Today, she was not just on a shopping trip, but also on a vital mission for Daddy. It made her stomach churn pleasantly to think about it.

"Now, I shall review my finances," Hannah declared grandly. This was a phrase that she'd heard Mummy say, jokingly, before she made out a shopping list.

Hannah pulled two purses out of her red shoulder bag. Her brown purse held her saved pocket money, and the black purse held three crisp ten-shilling notes.

She took out the notes and inspected them. They were very fine-looking. In a way, Hannah thought that they were prettier than whatever she might buy with them, though she knew that was not the sort of admission to make to a grown-up.

Hannah loved money. She gloated over each week's pocket money and was always on the lookout in the gutter for dropped halfpennies.

"Look after the pennies and the pounds will look after themselves," Hannah declared, pulling the arm rest into place and sitting tall, flapping her hand regally to a herd of cows as the train steamed past.

Sometimes, she liked to pretend she was Princess Elizabeth or Margaret Rose. She wondered what the princesses were doing today and whether they were going Christmas shopping, too.

Suddenly, the train whistled and Hannah realised that they were nearing Sulby. Hastily, she pulled down the window strap on the platform side.

"Grandma, Grandma!" she cried as the train steamed to a halt. "Here I am!"

The guard ran along the platform to ensure that Grandma got into the right carriage.

"All right now, little girl?" He smiled, and Hannah nodded politely.

Nevertheless, when he'd hurried off to blow his whistle, she muttered under her breath.

"I'm not a little girl. I'm almost nine."

Grandma, who was settling herself on the seat with her back to the engine, chuckled.

"You be glad you're a little girl, Hannah. Being a big girl's not much fun in this weather. Look at my chilblains!"

Hannah looked obediently at the pink lumps on Grandma's fingers, though she didn't think it was quite nice to display such things. Mummy said that Grandma was only happy when she had something to moan about, but that wasn't always so. Grandma could be jolly and cheerful when she liked.

Today was one of her cheerful days.

Grandma began to talk. In fact, but for a few moments when Hannah got a word in edgeways, Grandma talked non-stop all the way to Douglas.

She told Hannah who lived in each house alongside the track and when they'd moved there. She spoke about what she was going to buy, and what it had been like when she'd been a little girl. Then, the Christmas trains had been so jam-packed, you could hardly get on, let alone have a carriage to yourself like they had.

"Too many cars, today. Folks is too rich for their own good," she said firmly.

Hannah yawned, then hastily covered her mouth.

"Are you sleepy? Never mind, pet. Sure as herrings is bony, Douglas will wake you up." Grandma laughed, gathering her various bags. "Why look, Hannah, it's started to snow. Now that's real Christmassy."

"We won't get snowed in, will we, Grandma?" Hannah asked.

"No, not today, pet, though we might have a white Christmas yet. Now, get your bonnet fastened and your coat done up. My, that's a bonnie handbag. You're quite the lady!"

"It's one of Mummy's old bags," Hannah confided, as they got out of the carriage and were swept along by the rest of the good-humoured passengers.

"Keep hold of my hand, Hannah, child. There's no knowing what it'll be like in Strand Street."

HANNAH'S insides clenched as they hurried from the station and turned along the quay. Strand Street! The main shopping thoroughfare of Douglas town; how grand it sounded.

Just how grand it was Hannah soon discovered when they joined the merry bustle of Christmas shoppers thronging the narrow street; bright shop windows on every side, festively decorated cafés and restaurants tempting customers with delicious aromas of coffee and cooking.

Hannah was just thinking how long it had been since breakfast when Grandma abruptly steered her into a narrow lobby and up some stairs.

"A trip to Douglas wouldn't start right without a pot of tea," Grandma declared, leading her to one of several tables near a roaring fire. "I always come here before I get down to business."

"Do you?" Hannah asked. She was about to say more, but a waitress hurried up.

"Tea and scones for two, please," Grandma said. She gave Hannah an indulgent glance. "And a dish of jam."

She leaned across the table.

"We'll spoil ourselves, shall we, Hannah love?"

Hannah smiled. This was how she'd like life to be all the time — warm, waited on, her purse bulging with pennies and Christmas just around the corner.

She felt a sudden pang. She hadn't thought about Mummy for ages. Mummy had been feeling poorly that morning, and Auntie Jean had come to sit with her while Daddy was out.

As if reading her mind, Grandma leaned across the table.

"There'll be a new little brother or sister soon, Hannah."

"I know," Hannah whispered. Another pang smote her. How would she cope with a brother or sister when she was used to being the centre of attention?

"They'll look up to you," Grandma assured her.

Hannah looked at her curiously. How did Grandma know exactly what she was thinking?

"Pot of tea for two, scones and jam." The waitress set the things out with experienced swiftness.

"Thank you." Hannah smiled, and Grandma nodded her approval.

"The scones look good. Tuck in, Hannah, love. We've got lots to do after this."

Hannah didn't need encouraging. She tucked in.

AFTERWARDS, Hannah and Grandma visited several shops, where Grandma accumulated innumerable parcels. Hannah bought a striped tie for her father and a pretty scarf for her mother. After much deliberation, she chose a pair of woolly bootees with blue ribbons for the new baby, even though Grandma had suggested that yellow might be more sensible.

Hannah was pleased with her purchases, but surprised by how much they'd cost. Her purse was almost empty.

As they emerged into the street, she pulled on Grandma's hand.

"I have to get something else, but I don't know where to get it. It's something special for Mummy from Daddy, you see."

"Oh," Grandma said. "What is this special thing?"

"They're things, but they're private," Hannah murmured, looking round

Cushendun, Co. Antrim

A PICTURESQUE village at the mouth of the River Dun in North Antrim, Cushendun has long been a landing place and ferry point between Scotland and Ireland.

Visitors come to enjoy its long, sweeping beach and stunning coastal scenery, and the area is also of particular archaeological interest.

There's a wealth of holiday activities and facilities in the region, making this quiet corner a smart choice for a break.

J. CAMPBELL KERR.

rather uncomfortably.

Grandma chuckled.

"Go on, tell me."

"I'll whisper," Hannah said.

Grandma put her head down. Hannah spoke a few conspiratorial words.

"Oh, that's no problem," she said. "Come along, we'll get them now." She began to hurry the way they'd come, and then she noticed Hannah's face.

"Good heavens, child. You look all in. Shall we have dinner before we finish our shopping? Would you like that?"

"Yes, please, Grandma."

Meat pie and vegetables, and a sit down, restored Hannah, though she still felt bemused by the crowds and her head had begun to ache. There were so many people in Douglas. Somehow, when she'd imagined this day, it hadn't been like this at all.

It occurred to her, as she stared around, that if she were a princess, life might be like this all the time. In which case, she was glad she was not a princess. She'd rather be herself, Hannah Corkhill from Ramsey, Isle of Man.

"Now we'll get Daddy's present." Grandma winked as she counted the money for their bill, and gave Hannah a thrupenny to put under the plate for the waitress. "You must always do that, Hannah. These girls work hard for their money."

Hannah looked at the waitresses, rushing about laden with trays, and thought how clever they looked, and how tireless.

"I did that, when I was young," Grandma admitted. "My feet have never been the same since."

Hannah gazed wonderingly at Grandma. Had Grandma really ever been slim enough to slip between tables like that? It seemed impossible.

THE hosiery shop was quiet and rather refined. Hannah felt uncomfortable, but Grandma did the talking and soon they were looking at a selection of the most delicate nylon stockings Hannah had ever seen.

"How much did Daddy give you, pet?" Grandma asked, and Hannah delved into her red bag to find the special purse with the three crisp ten-shilling notes.

She pulled out her own purse with its few pennies, her handkerchief, a cough sweet, a comb and a pencil. She felt her face getting hot. Where was the black purse?

Feeling agitated, she tipped the bag upside down on the glass counter.

The assistant, who had appeared superior when they entered, began to look sympathetic, and that made Hannah feel worse.

"I must have lost it." She sniffed. "Oh, Grandma, I must have lost it."

"Well, there, there," Grandma said, looking a little put out. She felt in her own bag and found her purse and paid for a pair of sheer nylon stockings.

The assistant carefully wrapped the box and handed them over.

"I do hope the young lady finds the missing article, madam," the assistant said, as they gathered their belongings.

"So do I," Grandma replied a little grimly, and Hannah's eyes went all blurry with tears.

"I am so sorry, Grandma," she whispered, as they stepped out into the street.

"Never mind, lovey. Worse things happen at sea. Goodness, just look at the time. And it's snowing again. We'd best get a move on."

HANNAH held tightly to Grandma's hand as they headed back to the station, a walk that seemed much longer than when they'd arrived. Hannah felt wretched. Her feet hurt, her head hurt and worse than that was the ache of mortification in her chest.

"What carriage shall we take, Hannah, pet? Oh, I'm ready for a sit down. I'm fair exhausted."

Hannah looked at the numbers on the carriages.

"Number eight," she mumbled. It was the one she'd chosen that morning — eight because she was eight and a half and had thought herself grown up.

Now, she didn't feel grown up. Grown-ups didn't lose purses when they'd been trusted to buy something.

How could she tell Daddy? He called her his "big girl", but big girls who were trusted shouldn't lose things. Poor Grandma was out of pocket and so would Daddy be, because he'd have to pay Grandma back.

"There now, are you comfy?" Grandma gazed thoughtfully at Hannah. "You're tired, poppet. Cuddle close and have a sleep. Don't worry about that money. Your daddy won't be cross. These things happen."

Hannah closed her eyes, for she knew that tears were going to squeeze from them again. She felt utterly miserable. She had let herself down, and she'd let Daddy down. Was it because she had got "too big for her boots"? She'd heard that expression recently. Now, to her shame, she knew what it meant.

Hannah snuggled close to Grandma, but the arm rest was in the way. She pushed it up, and as she did so, she heard a soft thud as something dropped on the cushion beside her.

Through tear-filled eyes, she saw her lost purse lying on the worn moquette.

"Grandma! Look!" Hannah cried. "It must have got caught in the arm rest this morning."

"Is the money still there? Yes? Well, you *are* a lucky girl. Perhaps a Christmas angel was watching over you."

"Do you think so?" Hannah beamed. Then her face fell. "No, I was careless, Grandma, and I'm very sorry." She handed over the three crisp ten-shilling notes. "Thank you for paying for the stockings."

Grandma chuckled.

"You're a funny one, Hannah Corkhill, but you're a lovely granddaughter, and if your new brother or sister is half as nice as you I'll be a very lucky lady."

Hannah flushed. No-one had ever paid her such a nice compliment.

As the train gathered speed, and Hannah stared out of the window into the darkness, she thought over the happenings of the day. She'd been lucky all right, but she had also been careless. Perhaps she wasn't quite as capable as Daddy had thought?

* * * *

The next thing Hannah knew, Grandma was shaking her gently awake.

"I must get out now, Hannah. Only two stops to Ramsey, where Daddy will meet you. Thank you for being such good company. See you on Christmas Day!"

Hannah kissed Grandma. The door banged and the train steamed out of the station. Hannah sat up, smiling. Soon she'd be home.

As the train neared the inkpot house, Hannah lowered the window. The incoming air was biting, though the snow had stopped and the sky was punctured with bright stars.

"It's nearly Christmas," Hannah whispered to herself, as the train began to slow and she gathered her things. "I feel I've been away for ages. I wonder how Mummy is?"

The train stopped and Hannah fumbled with the door, stepping out on to the dark platform apprehensively amidst the package-laden shoppers.

"Hannah, Hannah!" Mick Corkhill came running towards her. "You've got a baby brother! What do you think of that?"

Hannah beamed.

"Oh, Daddy, I'm so glad!" She threw her arms around him. "It's been such a long day and I've missed you."

"I've missed you, too," her father cried. "Did you have a good time? Did you get the present for Mum?"

"Yes." Hannah nodded. She would admit her mishap later, but not now. Now, all that mattered was to get home and see Mummy and the baby.

As she and her father ran from the station, Hannah realised that, though it was very nice to go shopping and have pennies to spend, there were some things that money could not buy. Some things were much more precious than could be bought from any shop, even in Douglas.

Like a new baby.

No matter what might be in her Christmas stocking this year, nothing could ever be as exciting as a new baby brother! ■

The Beckoning Hills

Whenever I stayed with Grandma Brown,
In that friendly little northern town,
From my window tall green hills I'd see,
Hills that seemed to be beckoning me . . .
And then, one Sunday, Gran let me go
Off hiking, with Jimmy, and Mike, and Joe,
The boys next door, whom I'd come to know.

With our packets of sandwiches (mine were Spam,
Made with a spicy kind of ham),
And our bottles of water, off went we,
So light of heart, and so fancy-free.
And, what with the sunshine, the sky so blue,
The skylarks singing, the lovely view,
For me it was really a dream come true.

As we ran up the hill, there were sheep galore,
And flowers that I never had seen before,
Then we came to a stream, and oh, such fun
We had, as we paddled, and splashed in the sun.
All laughing, and noisy, and devil-may-care,
On that shimmering day, in the sparkling air,
Why, we were happy beyond compare!

And in my heart will the memory stay,
Until I can venture — who knows when? —
Over the hills, and far away,
To find the boy that I was then . . .
— *Kathleen O'Farrell.*

Let Nothing You Dismay...

by Caroline Cornish.

WHEN she asked me to babysit for her, a few days before Christmas, my granddaughter Emma was genuinely apologetic.

"I feel awful asking you, Gran," she said, looking guilty, "but Jim's been so looking forward to this evening. Laura, who usually comes, has a migraine . . . and I'll never find anyone else, so close to Christmas."

"It's perfectly all right," I assured Emma. "I don't mind a bit."

And it was true. Even with that momentous birthday approaching — what a word, octogenarian, it made me feel like a dinosaur — I was undaunted.

So, when evening came, I bundled up my knitting and sallied forth to Jim and Emma's, only a short walk from my bungalow. And there were the twins, Aaron and Abigail, sitting quietly watching a video, all bathed and ready for bed, like a pair of downy ducklings in their matching yellow pyjamas.

When Emma and Jim came down, looking so nice in their party gear, I was really pleased they hadn't been disappointed.

I knew what the rules were: up to bed when "The Lion King" was over, lights out in their bedroom as soon as they were in bed, but the landing light left on, for reassurance.

I foresaw a pleasant few hours to myself, watching TV while my busy

166

knitting needles clicked away, and my pretty amethyst jumper grew by inches.

About ten minutes after the taxi had borne Emma and Jim away, the TV screen went blank, and the lights failed. Our side of town was having a power-cut, the first one of the winter.

After a few shrieks of dismay, their video being only halfway through, the children were most helpful. I think they found it rather a lark.

"Mummy keeps some candles in a drawer in the kitchen," Abigail volunteered, so we groped our way out there and found them.

As I lit the candles — and it might have been some ancient rite I was

167

performing — their gentle glow illuminated the little faces watching me.

"I like candles," Aaron murmured. "They're sort of friendly."

I placed one on the hall table, at the foot of the stairs. The other one I was taking up to their bedroom.

But I couldn't leave two small children alone with a lighted candle, so I promised to stay with them until they were ready to drop off.

"Are you excited about Christmas?" I asked as I unrolled my knitting, and to my surprise they shook their heads, looking forlorn.

"Not all that much." Aaron sighed. "You see, it won't be very good this year. We're only having small presents! I can't have my Playstation, and Abigail can't have her doll's-house."

"Mummy and Daddy say we must wait till next year," Abigail chimed in .

"That sounds very sensible to me," I said briskly, for I knew how worried Jim and Emma had been, during Jim's spell of unemployment. Money had been really tight then.

"But small presents can be very nice, too, you know. And sometimes we treasure them even more than the expensive ones — especially if they're given with love."

In the candlelight, two little faces gazed at me doubtfully.

Then I had an inspiration. It wouldn't be as enthralling as "The Lion King", perhaps, but I could tell them a bedtime story, about Christmas long ago, when everything had been so utterly different . . .

Perhaps it was the candlelight that evoked those memories, but as I began to tell those little folk about my loveliest Christmas ever, the years seemed to roll away — all seventy of them . . .

IT had been a hard year for our family, the Ludlows, and now that a cruel winter had set in, it was doubly so. Father had fallen from a hayrick in the summer and hurt his back, so he was unable to work. If Mother hadn't taken in washing we might have starved.

We lived in a thatched cottage, whitewashed and half-timbered, pretty to look at, but with lots of disadvantages. The garden was our mainstay, though, with most of it given over to vegetables, and that was how Mother fed us.

However did Mother manage? Respectability was her watchword, which meant she never ran up bills (hence the use of candles, sometimes, to save money on the gas). We were always clean and tidy, held our heads up, and never let anyone know if we were hungry.

We all had our little jobs to do, of course, and mine was to help my sister Phyllis to carry the washing to and fro, in a big wicker basket with a handle at each end. Mother washed and ironed so beautifully, and most of the washing came from Mrs Summerfield, whose husband owned Summerfield's Store in town, and they had a cook and a maid.

The laundry was done in a stone copper in our scullery, and Mum had to get up early in the morning to light a fire under it. The scullery would soon be all hot and soapy and steamy as the washing boiled away.

As a little girl, I loved to see all those items, all colours of the rainbow, dancing and whirling and twirling halfway up to heaven in the wind. But what hard work it must have been for our gallant mother . . .

"It must have been awful then." Aaron sighed pityingly.

"Oh, no, it wasn't," I explained, "because life was simpler then, and we didn't expect so much. When I received a skipping rope on my birthday I was as happy as could be. Mind you, there was one special thing that I longed for, that particular Christmas — but I didn't have a hope of getting it."

THERE had been no Christmas spirit in the Ludlow household that year, I reminded them, for apart from Father being laid up, the larder was nearly bare, and we children were suffering from colds and chilblains.

There were five of us youngsters, Phyllis, Georgie, Harry, Baby Daisy and myself, Lucy, in the middle, and we just got on and made the best of things.

And then, one morning, when Mother was sorting out Mrs Summerfield's washing, she gave a great gasp. She'd found a pound note!

Never will I forget the look on her face as she stood there. And I've often wondered if she'd been tempted, just for a moment or two.

"A pound would have bought so much then," I told my great-grandchildren. "Nice food, and tea, and candles, and cough-mixture, perhaps something special for poor Dad, fretting up there in that dark, chilly bedroom. Oh, it would have meant so much to us, a whole pound to spend . . ."

But only for a moment did Mum hesitate.

"On with your coat, Lucy. You'll have to take this back to Mrs Summerfield. No-one can afford to lose a pound note."

So off I had to go — and it was such a horrible, bitterly cold morning. But it wasn't the walk I minded so much, it was having to wear that old grey coat, the only one I possessed.

It was a hand-me-down from Phyllis, who was much taller than me, and I was absolutely lost in it, and some of the children made fun of me, especially Nellie Hooper. I detested that Nellie Hooper, but I detested the coat even more. I longed for one that fitted me — a pretty coat, in a cheerful colour.

"I even sent a wish up the chimney to Santa Claus," I confessed to the twins (who looked very wise and knowing at the mention of that name), "but I knew it was hopeless. The most I could expect from him were the usual things in my stocking — an apple, orange, sugar-mouse, bright new penny, and perhaps a gingerbread man."

Anyway, I'd set off with a good grace, to please Mother, and her parting injunction rang in my ears all the way.

"Be sure to ask to see Mrs Summerfield herself, there's a good girl. Don't you go giving it to That Nancy."

That Nancy was the maid, a pretty girl, rather uppity in her ways. In summer we'd see her at local fairs and events, looking very superior, with a hat trimmed with poppies perched on her glossy black curls. The village lads regarded her with awe and admiration, but the grown-ups didn't like her.

AS I tapped on the kitchen door, I hoped Cook would open it, but, unfortunately, it was That Nancy who confronted me, very smart in her crisp white cap and apron. She asked me bluntly what I wanted.

"Please," I said nervously, "I have to see Mrs Summerfield. My mother said I must ask for her, as it's very important."

"*You* can't see Madam," she told me. "But you can give me a message for her, and I'll pass it on. It can't be all that important."

"But it is," I persisted. "It really is. And I must see Mrs Summerfield."

Tears were not far off — she was looking down on me as if I were an earwig.

"Don't be silly. Just give me the message. Madam's busy — and anyway, I can't be bothering her with all the ragtag and bobtail that comes to the door."

I couldn't believe what I was hearing. Surely I didn't deserve to be called that, shabby as I was, huddled in that dreadful old coat? Nor did my family either — not my brave mum, always up to her elbows in soap-suds, nor poor, suffering Dad. That Nancy was insulting us all.

"How dare you, Nancy Duckett!" I burst out. "How dare you call us that? You think you're so special, don't you — just because you've got a posh hat with poppies on . . ." And then the tears fell, trickling down my face.

"Whatever's the matter?"

Cook had come over to us, and behind her, tall and calm and dignified as a duchess, in a nice blue dress, was Mrs Summerfield.

"She asked to see you, Madam." Nancy looked deferentially at Mrs Summerfield. "Only I didn't want to bother you."

But Mrs Summerfield took charge. She drew me into that cosy kitchen with its enticing cooking smells, and smiled at me reassuringly.

"You're Mrs Ludlow's little girl, aren't you — Lucy, I believe?"

And then I brushed my tears away and handed her the pound note, explaining how Mum had found it. But I was still trembling with rage and misery.

"Please thank your mother for me, Lucy," Mrs Summerfield said, taking the money, "and tell her how grateful I am."

She went on to enquire about my father, and I told her he was still poorly, but

Village Skating-Party

Their warm winter woollies they donned
When icy winds chilled to the bone,
To trudge to the hard-frozen pond
Whence all the wild mallard had flown,
And brush off the snow,
Set lanterns aglow,
And skate to an old gramophone!

Old gentlemen, gallant and gay,
Waltzed round with an elegance rare;
Fat ladies in cosy array,
On ice, became lighter than air!
And those without skates
Just cheered on their mates,
Or came along only to stare.

Such innocent pleasure they knew —
No wireless or flickering screen,
But friendship, enduring and true,
To keep all their memories green;
Sweet peace in the air —
And no-one aware
They were making a Christmas-card scene!
*— **Brenda G. Macrow.***

longing to get back to work. And she was so sympathetic and understanding. Then she asked Cook to look after me, and suddenly I felt better.

"You poor little shrimp," Cook cried, "you're all pink with the cold."

And she gave me a mug of lovely hot cocoa, and a big slice of bread and honey before I started back home.

"Was Mrs Summerfield pleased?" Mum asked, and I was happy to tell her that Mrs Summerfield was really grateful.

I never mentioned That Nancy, but what she had said still rankled.

But next morning, in the chill light of day, That Nancy was forgotten, for we awoke to a sparkling world, all white and crystal-clear and magical. And very soon it was Christmas Eve, the start of a truly traditional white Christmas — and a day when one of my dearest wishes would be realised.

THAT afternoon we had a caller, Mr Timms, the Summerfields' gardener. He came on his bike, and was closeted with Mum in our tiny front room, always kept spick and span for visitors. When Mr Timms left, Mum called me in.

"What a lucky girl you are, Lucy. Such a lovely surprise . . . see what Mrs Summerfield's sent you! It belonged to Miss Charlotte, but she's grown out of it."

I stared and stared at what Mum was holding up. It was a coat — such a gorgeous, glowing shade of cherry-red, and as good as new. The collar was black velvet, and there was a row of little velvet-covered buttons down the front to match.

Tentatively, I reached out a finger to stroke the soft woollen material. In all my wildest longings, I'd never dreamed of such a beautiful coat.

"Well," Mother said, "aren't you going to try it on?"

So I slipped it on, and the most wonderful feeling crept over me . . . a feeling of such utter bliss and contentment that I knew I'd never be quite so happy again.

"What a perfect fit," Mum cried, almost as thrilled as I was.

"Oh, Mum, I feel just like a princess," I told her. Then I pressed my face against her pinafore, and wept tears of joy.

Although we knew what to expect in our stockings, we still awoke early next morning in happy anticipation, delving into them with glee. Then, after breakfast, when we'd each had a boiled egg, we went off to chapel.

Because I knew vanity was a sin, I tried hard not to feel proud in my pretty new coat, though I couldn't help hoping that Nasty Nellie would see me, and rub her gooseberry eyes in disbelief.

And when we came home, all exhilarated and hungry, the rabbit stew was simmering deliciously in the oven — and there was Father, who'd made the big effort to come down and have Christmas dinner with us!

He still looked frail, and his dear, kind face was gaunt, but it was wonderful to see him there, at the head of the table again.

But there was still more to come . . .

At teatime, with the candles lit and firelight flickering on the walls, Mum produced a big iced cake that Mrs Summerfield had sent, in appreciation of our mother's good work and reliability, she'd said.

It was the sort we children had hitherto only gazed at, wide-eyed and open-mouthed, in bakers' windows, with a holly-berry frill around it, Santa Claus and his sleigh in the middle, and *YULETIDE GREETINGS* written across it in gold. What shining eyes there were in that candle-lit kitchen!

Then, after tea, Dad fetched his fiddle off the front room wall.

"How about a bit of a dance? Come on, you little 'uns."

And as his merry music filled the air we all danced around him, even little Daisy, just feeling her feet, who clutched hands tightly with Phyllis and me, chuckling with delight. Oh, what high jinks we had that Christmas.

Small wonder then that I treasure the memory of it above all others — for there would never be another Christmas quite like that again.

BY the time I'd finished my narrative, the twins were almost asleep — and I suspected that I'd enjoyed the telling of it more than they had enjoyed hearing it . . . but what did it matter?

"What happened to that awful old grey coat?" Abigail asked drowsily.

"Funnily enough, it came in useful." I answered, smiling. "Dad insisted on going back to work, because everyone was so busy. It was lambing time, you see, and one day he brought home this wee orphan lamb for us to hand-rear."

"So you kept it warm in the coat," Aaron suggested, always interested in animals.

"Yes, we lined a box with the old coat, and put it in a corner of the kitchen, and Lambie was so snug there. We fed him from a baby's bottle, and he became quite a pet, dear little mite."

I felt gratified that I was able to round my story off so satisfactorily.

"Now, off to Dreamland, you two." I bent over the little sleepyheads, and kissed them, then crept downstairs, taking the candle with me.

And, would you believe it, just as I reached the hall the power was restored — so I was able to make myself a longed-for cup of tea. ∎

Printed and Published in Great Britain by D.C. Thomson & Co., Ltd., Dundee, Glasgow and London.

ISBN   1 84535 048 0
EAN 9 781845 350482

J. CAMPBELL KERR.